Fair-Weather
Friends

Also by ReShonda Tate Billingsley

Getting Even
With Friends Like These
Nothing But Drama
Blessings in Disguise
The Pastor's Wife
Everybody Say Amen
I Know I've Been Changed
Let the Church Say Amen
My Brother's Keeper
Have a Little Faith
(with Jacquelin Thomas, Sandra Kitt, and J. D. Mason)

Fair-Weather
Friends

ReShonda Tate Billingsley

Pocket Books
New York   London   Toronto   Sydney

Pocket Books
A Division of Simon & Schuster, Inc.
1230 Avenue of the Americas
New York, NY 10020

First Pocket Books trade paperback edition September 2008

POCKET and colophon are registered trademarks of
Simon & Schuster, Inc.

For information about special discounts for bulk purchases,
please contact Simon & Schuster Special Sales at 1-800-456-6798
or business@simonandschuster.com

Manufactured in the United States of America

10   9   8   7   6   5   4   3   2   1

Library of Congress Cataloging-in-Publication Data

Billingsley, ReShonda Tate.
   Fair-weather friends / ReShonda Tate Billingsley. — 1st Pocket Books
trade paperback ed.
      p. cm.
   Summary: When racism separates members of Good Girlz, a church-related
community service group, the girls must remember that what is on the
inside matters more than the outside, and while they may not be able to
remove the world's prejudices, they can change themselves.
   [1. Racism—Fiction. 2. Friendship—Fiction. 3. African
Americans—Fiction. 4. Hispanic Americans—Fiction. 5. High
schools—Fiction. 6. Schools—Fiction. 7. Christian life—Fiction.] I. Title.
PZ7.B4988Fai 2008
[Fic]—dc22
                                                                2008012951

ISBN-13: 978-1-4165-5876-7
ISBN-10:   1-4165-5876-4

For the founders,
Alpha Kappa Alpha
Delta Sigma Theta
Zeta Phi Beta
Sigma Gamma Rho

Acknowledgments

As always, I have to say thank you, God, for seeing me through yet another book. I also wanted to take a quick moment to say thank you to all of the people who have made the Good Girlz the success that it is. I never anticipated the books taking off like they did!

Thank you to LaShay Smith, who loves and nurtures the Good Girlz as if they were real. You're just as passionate about them as I am—so thanks so much!

To Tanisha Tate, who stepped up to the plate and helped a sister out (literally) when I needed it most. I can always count on you.

To my daughters, Mya and Morgan, thanks for telling everyone you know about the Good Girlz and sharing your time with "Mommy's other girls."

To my support system: my dear husband, Miron; Nancy; and Fay. God has blessed me to have such incredible people supporting my dream. Thank you, thank you, thank you.

Pat Tucker Wilson and Jaimi Canady, thanks for always being there as I bounce ideas off of you.

To my agent, Sara Camilli; editor, Brigitte Smith; and publicist, Melissa Gramstad—the Good Girlz wouldn't be what they are if it weren't for you!

Much, much love to the women of Alpha Kappa Alpha Sorority, Inc., who made my "real" sorority experience one that I will treasure for life. To the other sororities of the Divine Nine, thank you for giving our young women a sisterhood to be proud of.

As I travel the country, I have encountered some wonderful, wonderful librarians and booksellers, but I have to give a special shout-out to Stephanie Boyd and the Willard Library in Battle Creek, Michigan, the Tulsa City-County Library, the Houston Public Library, and all the other libraries that have had me out to visit.

My biggest thanks of all goes to you—the reader. I may not know you, but I appreciate you so much. Please continue to support the Good Girlz and make sure you check out the next book!

Much love,

ReShonda

1

Camille

These chicks were off the chain!

I couldn't do anything but stare in awe at the twelve girls on the auditorium stage. Not only did they look cute as all get-out in their tight black low-riders and pink satin T-shirts with "Theta Diva" spelled out in rhinestones, but they were doing moves I'd never seen before. We were at my school's step show. The Thetas were the third act, and they were turning the place out.

As a member of my high school's drill team, I can appreciate a good dancer, but these girls were dancing and stepping like they were starring in that *Stomp the Yard* movie. They had the crowd going wild.

One of my best friends, Alexis, must've been thinking the same thing because she leaned in to me and shouted over the thumping rap music, "Girl, what's the name of this group again?"

"They're called the Theta Ladies. It's a sorority at my

school," I responded as we stood with the crowd and applauded like crazy while they exited the stage.

Although the sorority was on campus at a lot of other high schools here in Houston, the Thetas had just started at my school last year. I'd seen the girls around campus, wearing their pink-and-white T-shirts, but I'd never paid them much attention. Until now.

"Gimme a break. They ain't all that," my other best friend, Jasmine, said as she turned up her nose. I ignored her. Jasmine always had something negative to say. Not many things impressed her and she always found something wrong with everything.

Jasmine had come a long way from when we first met her a year and a half ago, though. That's when we all joined the Good Girlz, a community service group formed by Rachel Jackson Adams, the first lady of this church in our neighborhood.

I know the name may sound a little hokey, but don't get it twisted. We aren't some Goody Two-shoes group. In fact, Miss Rachel started the group as part of a youth outreach program at Zion Hill Missionary Baptist Church, where her husband was pastor. Even though her daddy was a preacher, Miss Rachel was buck wild as a teenager; and now that she was grown, she wanted to do something to help teens who were headed down the wrong path. And boy, were we headed down the wrong path.

I was actually facing jail time when I hooked up with

the Good Girlz. It's almost unbelievable, since I had never been in any major trouble before that, but the dog who used to be my boyfriend had my nose wide open. Six months after me and Keith started going together, he got arrested for carjacking an old lady. He kept saying he didn't do it. I believed him, but he couldn't wait for justice to prevail so he broke out of jail. (We later found out he really didn't do it. It was his stepbrother.)

After he escaped, Keith had me hide him at my grandma's house. The thing was, I didn't even know he'd broken out. He told me they let him go. Anyway, the police eventually found him at my grandma's house, and that fool took off through a back window and left me to take the rap for hiding him.

So when the judge told me it was either jail or the Good Girlz, well, you can see that was a no-brainer. Let me just tell you, I'm too cute for jail. (People tell me all the time I look like a prettier version of Kyla Pratt, that girl who played on the TV show *One on One*.)

It's a good thing I joined the Good Girlz because the police later found Keith hiding out at his baby mama's house. Did I mention that I didn't know he had a baby? Or a baby mama? So, I probably would've been in prison for real for killing him if it wasn't for the Good Girlz.

"Look how they're strutting around like they're all that." Jasmine's voice snapped me out of my thoughts.

I grinned as I watched the Thetas walk down the aisle.

Everyone was stopping them and giving them props. "They are all that," I said, my voice full of admiration.

"Really, they're not," Jasmine snarled.

I blew her off because Jasmine was my girl, funky attitude and all. Miss Rachel had made Jasmine join the Good Girlz after breaking up a fight between her and this boy named Dedrick. At six feet tall, Jasmine wasn't anybody you wanted to mess with. Just ask Dedrick. She had beat him like he stole something just because he was teasing her.

Jasmine has actually toned down some of her mean ways over the last year and a half. Although you'd never know it by the way she was sitting over there with her nose all turned up.

"I didn't know they even had sororities in high school," Alexis said.

Alexis was the rich girl of the group. Her dad is some big-time businessman, and her family has beaucoup money. She resembled Beyoncé (and she didn't hesitate to let you know it) and was always dressed in the tightest clothes, looking like she had just stepped off the cover of a magazine. But she's so cool that her bourgie ways don't bother me. Most of the time anyway.

I turned my attention back to Alexis, since she was just as hyped as I was.

"Yeah, lots of high schools have sororities," I said.

"Have you ever thought about joining?" the fourth

member of our group, Angel, leaned in and asked. She'd been so quiet I'd almost forgotten she was there. But that was Angel's nature. She was the sweet, quiet one of the group. Getting pregnant at fifteen had made her grow up pretty fast, especially because her baby's daddy was this triflin' boy named Marcus, who didn't even claim their daughter, Angelica. I loved Angel, and her daughter was so adorable, but I wouldn't trade places with her for anything in the world.

"I think it would be cool to be a Theta," Alexis said wistfully. "But they don't have them at my school."

Alexis was the only one of us that didn't go to Madison High School. She went to a private school called St. Pius on the other side of town.

"I told you about that new rule the school district has that lets students participate in extracurricular activities at another school if your school doesn't offer it," I said. "So, you could join the Thetas at our school."

"For real?" she asked, wide-eyed.

I nodded as the next sorority made their way on to the stage. Sure, I'd watch them perform; but for me, the Thetas had already stolen the show.

2

Camille

I couldn't stop talking about the Theta Ladies. As a matter of fact, the whole school was talking about them. Surprisingly, they didn't win first place in the step show. They'd come in second behind a sorority from Booker T. Washington High School. Still, after the step show, the boys had been all over them like they were celebrities or something.

I'd filled in our fellow Good Girlz member, Tameka Adams (she was Miss Rachel's niece and had joined the group about six months after we started). I'd told her all about the show and now she was just as hyped as I was, and sick that she'd missed it in the first place.

"Dang, I didn't know the Thetas had it goin' on like that," she said. "I can't believe I missed it."

"You ought to quit sneaking out of the house. Then maybe you wouldn't be on punishment all of the time." I laughed.

"Now see, you asking too much," she joked.

Even though me, Jasmine, Alexis, and Angel weren't as close to Tameka as we were to one another, she was still cool and I was glad to see she was worked up about the Thetas, too.

Jasmine had gotten tired of hearing me rave about them, but Angel and Alexis were still excited. Me and Angel were rehashing our favorite parts of the show to Tameka as we made our way into the pizza line in the school cafeteria.

"Hey, isn't that the girl who was leading the Thetas' step team this weekend?" Angel whispered as we grabbed our trays. I looked up to see who she was talking about. She was motioning toward a tall, pretty, mocha-skinned girl who was at the front of the line.

"Yeah. Her name is Raquelle. She's on the drill team with me," I replied.

"Isn't that Tori Young next to her? She wasn't in the show, was she?" Angel asked.

"I didn't see her, but maybe she was in the back or something," I answered.

I was glad that Jasmine wasn't here. She usually ate lunch with us but she had to take a makeup test today. Jasmine and Tori didn't get along. Then again, there weren't too many people who Jasmine *did* get along with. But Tori and Jasmine were definitely like oil and water. Mainly because of Donovan, Jasmine's ex-boyfriend. He was in college now, but when he transferred here from New Orleans after

Hurricane Katrina, Tori had set her sights on him. Only he was trying to get with Jasmine and wouldn't give Tori the time of day. She definitely couldn't appreciate that. She and Jasmine had almost come to blows several times behind him.

"I knew she was a Theta," I told Angel as we paid for our pizza. "But I just found out yesterday that she's actually the president."

"Wow. They look so cute in those jackets," Tameka said, admiring the thin pink satin jackets with the word Theta on the front and a white poodle, which was their mascot, on the back. It was hot outside, but inside, our buildings were always freezing, so they didn't look out of place in their jackets.

"Are you guys going over there?" Tameka said.

I debated for a minute. "Maybe I'll just say hi as we pass by."

Tameka looked at her watch. "Dang, I have got to get to detention. I wanted to go talk to them."

"Girl, you'd better go," I said. "You know Mr. Matthews said he was going to add two more weeks of detention if you were late again."

Tameka huffed like life was so unfair as she told us bye and headed out of the lunch room.

We made our way toward our normal seats in the back of the cafeteria. I caught eyes with Raquelle as we passed the Theta table. I didn't want to be jockin' anybody, but

I did want to let them know how tight their show had been.

"Hey Raquelle," I said, stopping in front of their table. She was sitting with Tori and several other girls. All of them were wearing the Theta jackets. "I just wanted to tell you all that show you did this weekend was off the hook."

Raquelle smiled. "Thanks."

"And you all were definitely robbed," I continued. "Everybody knows you guys should've won first place."

She looked at the other girls and giggled. "Tell me about it."

"Isn't your name Camille?" one of the girls sitting beside Raquelle asked me.

"Yeah, it's Camille Harris. And this is my friend, Angel Lopez," I said, pointing to Angel, who waved meekly.

"You're on the drill team, aren't you?" another girl asked, all but ignoring Angel.

I nodded.

"Well, I'm Lynn. I'm vice president of the Thetas." Lynn pointed to the other four girls. "And this is Constance, Claudia, Alisha, and Tori."

"Oh, I know Camille very well," Tori snidely remarked.

I'd been around a couple of the times Tori had gotten into it with Jasmine so she definitely knew who I was. I smiled anyway. I didn't have a beef with Tori and I wasn't about to start now.

"Do you wanna sit with us?" Raquelle asked.

My mouth almost hit the floor. I knew the sorority girls could get a little snooty and they really didn't like anyone invading their clique. So I was thrilled that they wanted us to sit with them.

"Sure, we'd love to sit with you guys," I said.

Me and Angel sat down in two empty seats across from Raquelle. I couldn't be sure, but it looked like Tori and Claudia shot Angel a crazy look. It made me uncomfortable for a minute, but then I told myself I was just imagining things.

"So how long have you guys been Thetas?" I asked as I bit into my pizza.

"We all joined last year when we started the organization here at Madison," Lynn said.

"Do you all practice a lot to be able to step like that?" I continued.

Lynn smiled. "We do. But there is so much more to us than stepping. We actually do a lot of community service. You should check out our MySpace page and see what we're all about."

"I'll definitely do that."

I wrote down their MySpace address on the back of my geometry folder.

We talked and laughed the rest of the lunch period. I know a lot of people thought the Thetas were snobs, but I really liked them and we seemed to click.

I was kinda bummed when the bell rang, signaling the end of lunch. We had been hitting it off so much, I hated to see it end.

"Well, I gotta go. I got a test in Chemistry next period," Lynn said as she stood up. "Camille, it was nice meeting you. I've seen you around school but I didn't know you were so cool."

I smiled and waved good-bye to her and the other girls. Even Tori had warmed up to me, and smiled as she walked off.

I turned to Angel. "That was so cool," I said.

"For you, maybe," Angel replied, standing up and grabbing her tray.

I stood up, too. "What do you mean?"

Angel turned toward me. She had a disgusted look on her face. "Am I invisible? Nobody said two words to me the entire time."

I tried to laugh it off. But now that I thought about it, no one had really talked to Angel. It was probably just because she was so quiet.

"You weren't talking either," I said, playfully pushing her shoulder. Even though Angel was cute with her long, jet-black hair, olive-colored skin, and light brown eyes, she definitely lacked in the confidence department. The Thetas probably just picked up on that. "You know you're all shy and stuff. They talk so much, they probably didn't even pay you any attention."

"Exactly," she snidely replied.

"I didn't mean it like that. You know it takes you a minute to warm up to people."

She shrugged as she walked over and tossed her plate in the trash. "I guess. I mean, they are cool and all, but I'm not getting a good vibe from them."

I followed her and threw my trash away as well. "Come on, you're starting to sound like Jasmine. I think you're overreacting. They just need to get to know the Angel we all know and love."

She finally smiled. "I guess you're right."

I wrapped my arm through hers as we made our way through the crowd of students filing out of the cafeteria. "I know I am. And now more than ever I'm sure about it."

"Sure about what?"

I dropped her arm, looked at her, and grinned. "We need to be Thetas."

She turned up her lips. "Yeah, right."

"I'm serious."

Angel looked like she was thinking about it. "That would be tight, wouldn't it?"

"It would be especially tight if me, you, Jasmine, Alexis, and even Tameka were all Thetas."

Angel nodded. "It would be great to be in a sorority." The smile suddenly left her face and she looked at me skeptically. "Alexis, I can see. Even Tameka. But good luck getting Jasmine to go for the idea."

I smiled slyly. "You just leave that to me. I'll get Jasmine to come around."

Angel shrugged like she'd believe it when she saw it. Despite my confidence, I knew getting Jasmine to warm to the idea of joining the Thetas would be easier said than done.

3

Jasmine

I slammed my locker shut and looked at Camille like she was crazy.

"Don't say no yet," she pleaded.

I pulled my thick, honey brown hair back in my signature ponytail. I tried wearing it down like Camille was always buggin' me to, but it was too hot on my neck. Even though it was September it was still burning hot, at least to me. That's why I couldn't do anything but shake my head as the Thetas walked past me in their jackets.

"Please, don't say no," Camille repeated.

I stared at her. "No, *you* just say no to those drugs you must be on if you think for one minute I'm trying to be in some sorority."

I know Camille could tell by the look on my face that I wasn't even trying to hear her. Sure, I'd gotten a lot nicer over the last year, but I didn't ever see myself being some sorority girl.

"Come on, Jasmine, hear me out," she whined.

"Save your breath, Camille. It ain't happening," I said, since she obviously wasn't getting the picture. Picking up my backpack, I flung it over my shoulder and made my way out to the front of the school. I ignored Camille's pleas as I looked around for Angel. I spotted her coming out of the front office building.

"Angel!" I called out to her. We were all supposed to be meeting Alexis after school for one of our Good Girlz mentoring sessions with some girls from nearby Dowling Middle School.

I stayed two steps in front of Camille as I made my way over to Angel.

"Would you slow down and listen?" Camille said; she caught up with me just as I made it to Angel.

"Listen to what?" Angel asked. She was dressed really cute in a khaki miniskirt with some beige leggings, black Converse hi-tops, and a beige T-shirt. Her long black hair was tied loosely on her back.

"Listen to Camille talk crazy, that's what," I replied.

Camille put her hands on her hips and cocked her head. "What is so crazy about joining the Thetas?"

I shook my head as I looked down the street for Alexis. "You can join all you want. There ain't nothing those uppity sorority girls can do for me."

"They aren't uppity," Camille protested.

"Yes, they are," I replied.

"We had lunch with them yesterday," Angel added. "They really aren't that bad."

I sighed, not believing I was even having this conversation.

"So you see them shake their butts on stage, now all of a sudden you want to be a member?" I asked.

Camille exhaled loudly like I was really frustrating her. "It's not that at all. I mean, I'd been seeing them around school and stuff but I never really paid them much attention. But after they brought down the house at that step show, I just started talking to them."

"And let me guess," I interrupted, rolling my eyes. "You now think they're the greatest thing since sliced bread?"

Camille folded her arms across her chest, pouting. "Why you gotta be so negative?"

I just stared at her. "Camille, get real, okay? You watch these girls perform one time, and now they're supposed to be all that and a bag of chips."

"It's about more than being in step shows. They do stuff in the community and everything."

Camille was really getting on my nerves. "As if we need to do any more in the community. Hello!" I pointed down the street toward the middle school. "We're getting ready to go do community service right now. We don't need to join a sorority to do that."

"Jasmine, all I'm saying is think about it."

I let out a long, exasperated sigh. "Okay." I paused a

minute and put my finger to my head like I was thinking, then looked at Camille. "Thought about it, and the answer is still no."

"I don't know, Jaz," Angel chimed in. "It might be worth looking into. I kinda like the Thetas."

Camille broke out in a huge smile. "And the good thing is I called Alexis last night and she's game. Even Tameka is in."

"Well, y'all can be game without me because I'm not tryin' to be in a stupid sorority."

"Why does it have to be stupid? Huh, Jasmine?" Camille asked.

I rubbed my eyes. I knew Camille. She was not going to let up on this issue. I know I have gone along with a lot of things, but this whole "let's join a sorority" thing? I definitely wasn't feeling it.

"Why do they have sororities in high school anyway? I thought that was just for college," I snapped. "The whole idea is dumb."

"Girl, please. High school sororities are everywhere now. And they're the thing to be involved in," Camille said.

"Oh, so now we need to be in a sorority to prove we somebody?" I looked at my watch, then down the street, wishing Alexis would hurry up.

Camille stuck out her bottom lip. She could be so spoiled sometimes when she didn't get her way. "You make it sound so crazy," she finally said.

"That's because it is!"

She was just about to say something else when C. J., this chocolate-skinned boy I used to have a crush on, walked up. He was dressed like Kanye West in a bright orange vest, white T-shirt, and white pants. He actually looked really cute, although I'd never tell him that because he used to call me Grape Ape when we first met because I was so tall. But now he'd caught up to me in height and had the nerve to flirt with me. Still, I wasn't giving him the time of day.

"What's up, ladies?" He turned toward me. "Hey, Jasmine. You lookin' good today, girl."

I rolled my eyes. C. J. had been playing games since I first met him. One minute he was calling me names, the next he was mackin' like he wanted me to be his girl or something. I didn't have time to play games with him. He made me sick. Sometimes. If only he wasn't so dang cute.

"Whatever, C. J.," I muttered.

"We were just telling Jasmine why she should join the Thetas," Camille said. I knew what she was doing, trying to get C. J. in on the push to get me to join, and I couldn't appreciate that.

"Oh, that's what's up," C. J. said, a big grin crossing his face. "I can see you as a Theta Lady. You're hot just like them. But I don't know if you joining is such a good idea."

Camille frowned. "And why not?" she asked.

Even I was a little curious as to why he'd said that.

C. J. stroked his chin. "Because if Jasmine becomes a

Theta, I'm gon' have to fight the dudes off and I'll never get a chance." He stepped closer to me, his gaze burrowing into mine. "So I guess I don't want her to join for selfish reasons."

"Oh, gimme a break," Camille playfully groaned.

I couldn't help but smile, even though I was trying not to. I was also trying not to let my butterflies show because I didn't want C. J. to think he had my nose all wide open and stuff.

"Well, I gotta go. I have to get to band practice," C. J. said. "I'll talk to you later, Jasmine."

"No, you won't," I replied. He just smiled like he knew one day he'd break me down. Like that would ever happen. At least that's what I told myself.

We watched C. J. walk off just as Alexis pulled up, yapping away on her iPhone. She was the only person I knew who had one. Shoot, she was the only person I knew who could even afford one.

"Hey, girls," Alexis said, ending her phone conversation.

We all spoke and Camille immediately began filling Alexis in as we piled into her BMW. She, of course, was completely into trying out for the Thetas.

The three of them giggled incessantly as we made our way toward the middle school. I really had tuned them out until I heard Camille say, "Even C. J. thinks Jasmine should be a Theta."

I popped back into the conversation. "Like I care what C. J. thinks."

"You know you care," Camille teased. "And just think how cute he'll think you are wearing that pink and white," she added.

I sighed and stopped fighting. Maybe it was seeing C. J. Maybe it was just Camille finally wearing me down. Either way, I found myself saying, "Fine, I'll go check out the Thetas. But I'm not making any promises."

Camille squealed as she threw her arms around my neck and tried to hug me. "Yes! This is going to be so cool!"

I pushed her away. "Get off me!" But she could tell I wasn't mad.

She laughed then said, "I promise you won't regret this."

Camille just didn't know. I was regretting it already.

4

Jasmine

"I so cannot believe I'm doing this." I stared at myself in the mirror in the girls' bathroom. I had to admit that I was looking pretty cute in Alexis's black designer suit. The suit would probably swallow her now since she'd dropped six dress sizes, but it fit me perfectly since she'd had her housekeeper Sonya take it in. Shoot, it actually looked good on me. The skirt was a whole lot shorter on me that I imagine it was on Alexis but it still looked like it was made for me.

"I'm just glad you agreed to go," Camille said, fluffing out her spiral curls.

"It's not like you left me much choice," I mumbled. "You dang near put a gun to my head."

"Oh, stop being a drama queen. I simply explained to you all the reasons why you should consider joining the Thetas."

I added some MAC Lipglass, then responded. "Yeah, like you're their personal recruiter or something."

"Well, I'm just glad she got you to warm to the idea," Angel said.

"Yeah, we have to agree that we're all in this together or none of us are in it, okay?" Alexis said.

Camille and Angel nodded. Me? I just grunted, but I guess they took that for a yes because no one gave me a hard time.

"Does that little all-in-it-together pact include Tameka?" I smiled slyly, knowing that it probably should but it didn't. Even though we were cool with Tameka, we really could take her or leave her.

"Yes, of course it does," Camille replied. I could tell she was lying.

"Where is Tameka anyway?" Alexis asked.

"She had tutoring so she said she's going to meet us there," Camille answered.

Alexis shrugged like it didn't really matter.

Angel put the last of her makeup into her purse. "Wouldn't it be great if we all made it in?" she said as she made her way over to wait by the door.

"What do you mean *if*?" Camille asked. "Don't you mean *when*?"

Angel and Alexis giggled. On the other hand, I still wasn't feeling this whole idea. There was something about the sorority girls that just wasn't sitting right with me. But I guess it was too late now. We were getting ready to go into the interest meeting, and I'd already promised Camille that I would fill out an application.

"Come on, the meeting starts in five minutes," Alexis said, looking at her watch. She took part in a work-study program at her school that allowed her to skip her last two classes and go to work. Those people at her school should've known she wasn't working anywhere. But I guess you can do stuff like that when you're rich: Alexis came straight here so she could be on time for the meeting. Work wasn't even an afterthought for her.

"Do we really need to be the first ones there?" I asked as I headed to the door. "Dang."

"Would you stop complaining and come on," Alexis said.

We filed out of the bathroom and into the classroom where the Thetas were having their meeting. The room was packed with a bunch of wannabes so I guess I didn't have to worry about being one of the first ones there. Tameka was already seated in the front row. Talk about being excited. You'd think she was about to win the lottery or something the way she was cheesin'.

I recognized a lot of girls from around school. I had no idea any of them were even halfway interested in being in a sorority. But I'm sure they were saying the same thing about me.

"I'm going to need you to lose the attitude," Camille

leaned in to me and whispered as we walked to the back of the room.

I caught myself. I didn't realize I was scowling with my nose turned up.

"I'm cool," I said. I really was going to try and have a good experience. Since my girls were so excited about it, I was hoping I would warm to the whole idea. And who knows, maybe it would turn out to be okay.

The meeting got under way and we played a couple of games to break the ice and get to know one another. The games were actually fun. One of them required us to introduce ourselves to someone new and find out something unique about them.

After about ten minutes, me and most of the other girls had loosened up and we all were having a really good time.

I almost died when Tori Young walked to the front of the room and introduced herself as the president of the Theta Ladies. I could hang it up. Tori couldn't stand me. I couldn't stand her. I had a better chance of getting struck by lightning than getting accepted. I almost got up and walked out. Camille must've known what I was thinking because she squeezed my hand.

"It's no big deal," she whispered.

"For you, maybe. You know she hates my guts." I shook my head. "I knew I shouldn't have agreed to this."

If Tori hadn't already begun talking, I probably

would've gotten up and left the room. But since she was, I stayed put.

After Tori finished, another girl named Lynn got up and started talking about their history, when they were started, and the purpose of the group. Another girl followed her and talked about how the sorority wasn't all about stepping and dancing and how they tried to focus a lot on doing community service. Camille shot me an "I told you so" look. I smiled back at her and I could tell she was glad to see me relaxing a bit.

I had put Tori out of my mind and was now focused on Mrs. Lane, an English teacher and the Theta advisor. She was telling us about how we didn't have to worry about hazing, because it was against their rules. Thank goodness, 'cause I definitely wasn't with that.

"So, are there any questions?" Tori asked after they had all finished with their presentations.

A girl in the front row raised her hand. "Yes, I'd like to know if being in your organization will help me get into a sorority when I get into college."

Tori smiled like she was used to people asking that. "We aren't really affiliated with any of the national college sororities, but we do have a lot of the same ideas and principles. And we'd like to think we're sort of a training ground to prepare you for when you *do* get to college," she replied.

Seemingly satisfied with that answer, the girl nodded.

Tori took a few more questions, including one from this girl who was known around school as Funky Mona because she always smelled like rotten fish. I could tell from the look on Tori's face that Mona had about as much chance as I did of ever becoming a Theta Lady.

After the question-and-answer session, we all got applications to fill out. Tori walked over and personally handed me mine.

"Jasmine, I know we have a rocky history," she sweetly said. "But I want you to know that's all in the past. And I hope you don't let that keep you from deciding to apply to our wonderful organization."

I know shock was written all over my face. I never would've expected that from her.

"Ummm, thanks," was all I could reply.

She flashed another smile before walking off to talk to some other girls.

"See, if that's not proof you need to be a Theta, I don't know what is." Camille had crept up behind me and was now grinning widely.

I playfully rolled my eyes. Maybe Tori had changed and this wouldn't be so bad after all. Camille looked like she wanted to scream for joy when I sat down and began filling out my paper.

"So, now what?" I asked after we all turned in our applications and were leaving the meeting.

Camille smiled. "Now we wait for our invitation to join, then we become Theta Ladies."

I sighed, trying not to burst her bubble. She seemed like she had this all figured out. But my gut was still telling me things weren't going to go as smoothly as Camille had planned.

5

Camille

$\mathcal{M}$y eyes scanned the note in my hands. I'd found it stuffed inside my locker. It read:

Meet at Brentwood Park. Seven P.M. sharp! Wear black clothes and white tennis shoes!

The note was written on plain white paper and I wondered who wrote it. Just then Jasmine and Angel walked up.

"By the look on your face I see you got the same note we did," Jasmine said, unenthusiastically.

"Yeah, who do you think it's from?" I asked, reading it again. It had been a week since the Theta interest meeting and we were supposed to get a formal invitation to join, not some anonymous letter in our locker. Which is why I wasn't sure about it.

"It's from your local neighborhood welcoming committee," Jasmine replied sarcastically. "I swear, you can be so slow sometimes. It's from the Thetas, girl. I don't know what they have planned but I ain't meeting nobody at no park."

I turned the note over in my hand as reality set in. "Come on, Jasmine, don't be like that. If you are going to be accepted into the Theta Ladies you've got to have a better attitude than that."

"Look, this was you and Alexis's idea in the first place. I'm only going along with this nonsense because y'all are my girls," Jasmine said.

"Angel, you're being really quiet. What do you think? Are you going to go?" I asked her.

Angel, who looked like she had been deep in thought, shrugged. "I guess so, but I'm not gonna lie, I am a little nervous. We haven't even been accepted yet, and already they're trying to scare us."

I was about to respond when my purse began blaring the song "I'm a Flirt." I dug out my cell phone, then glanced at the caller ID. "It's Alexis," I said. "I wonder if she knows about the meeting. Hey, girl," I said, after I pushed the Talk button.

Alexis immediately began rambling. "Girl, I just got the strangest text message to meet at Brentwood Park at seven. I think it's from the Theta Ladies."

"We know. We got the same message, but your scaredy-cat friends over here don't want to go," I told her as I cut my eyes at Angel and Jasmine.

"Well, tell them that they are going whether they like it or not. Remember, we said we were all in this together. So . . . I'll see you guys at six fifty-nine. I gotta go, the tardy bell just rang and I'm late," Alexis said quickly as she hung up.

At exactly 6:59, me, Jasmine, Alexis, Tameka, and Angel walked up to the park. We immediately saw nine other girls, all lined up, all in black. Tori and Claudia were yelling in their faces. All of a sudden, Tori looked up and saw us.

"Well, thank you for joining us, ladies," she snidely remarked. "You're late. Get in line."

I glanced at my watch. "But I thought the note said seven. It's just now seven."

Tori raised her eyebrows, then walked over to me. She got so close I could smell the fruity apple Jolly Rancher she was sucking on.

"Number one, little girl," she spat, "don't ever talk back to me. Number two, and listen to me when I say this, to be early is to be on time, to be on time is to be late, and to be late is totally unacceptable! Now get . . . in . . . line!"

We scrambled into line next to the other girls. Shocked doesn't even begin to describe how I was feeling. They had all been so nice at the interest meeting. And even Raquelle, who was on the drill team with me and pretty cool, was standing there with her nose turned up at us.

I glanced over at Jasmine, who was biting down on her

bottom lip, something she did when she was trying to calm herself down. I knew she couldn't appreciate having anyone, especially Tori, screaming at her.

"I knew Tori was just frontin', trying to act all nice," Jasmine hissed at me.

I didn't respond as I began listening to the girls barking orders at us.

For the next thirty minutes we had to do push-ups and sit-ups, and run laps. From the look on Jasmine's face, I could tell she wasn't feeling this whole scene at all. She looked like she would punch someone in the jaw if they said anything to her. I thought about pulling her to the side to try to calm her down, but knowing Jasmine, she wouldn't think twice about going off on me, friend or no friend. I might even end up being the person who got punched.

As we were running the last of our five laps around the park's track, Jasmine caught up to me, Tameka, and Alexis.

"Y'all ~~busta owe me big~~ for this one. I didn't sign up for all of this. If I wanted to work out, I would go get a membership at 24-Hour Fitness," she said, panting, as she jogged alongside us.

"Quit complaining. It's really not that bad," Tameka said, and she took off, leaving us in her dust.

"Yeah," Alexis replied as we all slowed down just a bit. "We're all tired—well, most of us," she added, eyeing

Tameka's overzealous behind, "but it's almost over. Would it make you feel better if I promised to stop and buy us all ice cream on the way home?"

"No, it wouldn't. What? Am I five years old or something? You offering to buy me ice cream." Jasmine stopped and bent over to catch her breath.

"Come on," I said, pulling her arm. She continued jogging, but it was obvious she wasn't happy.

"Ladies, you must need an extra lap since you've got enough energy to talk!" Tori screamed as we passed her. "Jasmine, it probably wouldn't hurt you to do an extra lap anyway."

Uh-oh. That was a big mistake. Before I could say anything to her, Jasmine had stopped in her tracks and did a quick about-face.

"Oh, this girl has lost her mind," Jasmine said as she marched back toward Tori.

I knew if I didn't do something quick, this would turn into something very ugly and none of us would ever stand a chance of being Theta Ladies. By the time I reached Jasmine, the rest of the girls had noticed her stomping toward Tori and had stopped running to see what was going on.

Jasmine got up in Tori's face. "No you did not just go there. Girl, I will—"

"Jasmine!" I yelled. "Let me talk to you for a minute." I looked at her and pleaded with my eyes to please not say anything else. She must have picked up on the desperation in my face because she slowly backed away, never taking her eyes off of Tori.

"Yeah, Camille, get your little pit bull under control before she gets herself hurt." Tori was talking all tough, but I could tell she was afraid of what Jasmine might do.

"Well, if it isn't the Theta Ladies and the wannabe Theta Ladies." We all turned toward the husky voice that had literally saved Tori from getting a beat-down.

It was this guy named Vincent, the president of the fraternity at my school, Gamma Men. They were the big brothers to the Thetas. He was surrounded by a group of boys, who were all dressed in white T-shirts and black jeans. I'd heard they were having a line and judging from the scared-looking boys standing behind Vincent, the rumors were true.

"My boys here are on a scavenger hunt," Vincent said, pointing to the eight dudes behind him. "And they need some Theta help."

Tori grinned flirtatiously as she strutted over to Vincent. "And just how can my girls be of service?"

Vincent licked his lips and grinned back. "My boys here have been ordered to get a pair of Theta—or wannabe Theta—panties."

Tori busted out laughing. "Boy, you are so stupid." She looked over at the other Theta members. They were laughing, too.

"I say do it," Claudia offered.

"Me, too," Constance added. "As long as it's some wannabe panties."

Tori turned back to Vincent and slowly nodded. "Cool. We can do that." She turned back to us. "Jasmine, go in the bathroom and take off your drawers so you can give them to the Gammas," she said, fighting back laughter.

Jasmine looked at Tori like she'd lost her mind.

"Are you crazy?" Jasmine replied. "That's nasty."

The smile left Tori's face. She rolled her eyes then pointed a finger in Jasmine's face. "Look, I'm about sick and tired of you always having something to say. Give him your funky panties. Now!"

Jasmine put her finger right back in Tori's face. "I ain't giving him nothing, especially not my panties! Give him yours. Shoot, everybody else done had 'em."

Several people's eyes grew wide, including mine, at Jasmine's dig at Tori's reputation for being loose.

"Jasmine, it's no big deal," Tameka interrupted. I knew she was trying to keep this from blowing out of control.

Jasmine spun around. "No! This is stupid. Explain to me how giving somebody my underwear builds sisterhood. How does that make us better? Is that what the Thetas are about? Huh?"

Everyone got silent as Jasmine went off on her tirade.

"The running, the push-ups. None of it makes sense!"

"You know what?" Tori finally said as she glared at Jasmine. "You are really getting on my nerves."

"You know what?" Jasmine coldly replied. "The feeling's mutual."

"Hey." Lynn anxiously tugged at Tori's arm. "Isn't that Mr. Washington, the chemistry teacher?" She was pointing at a man jogging toward us on the track.

Tori studied him for a minute, then quickly turned to us and said, "Y'all, act natural."

We tried to stand around casually.

"Just act like we're talking," Tori whispered as Mr. Washington slowed his jog.

"Hello, ladies." He looked at Vincent and the other guys. "And gentlemen. What are you doing out at the park so late?"

"Just hanging out," Tori quickly said.

I know we all looked suspicious. I was nervously digging my foot in the gravel. Angel and Alexis were playing with their fingernails and the other nine girls wore guilty expressions. Tameka was the only one of us who didn't look like she was trying to hide something.

Mr. Washington eyed us skeptically. "And you're hanging out in all black? As hot as it is?" he asked.

"No, we were practicing for a step show. And we have the black on because we were just trying to see how the outfits would look," Tori said.

"Oh, okay. Well, you all be careful out here. And stay

out of trouble." He nodded knowingly before jogging away.

As soon as he took off, we all breathed a sigh of relief.

"Okay, that was close," Lynn said after he was gone. "We could've gotten in so much trouble. I think we need to call it a night."

"But we're not finished with them," Tori whined.

"Y'all do what you want. We're out of here," Vincent said as he motioned for his boys to scram. "I graduate in May. I ain't trying to get in no trouble."

"Tori"—Lynn put her hands on her hips—"do you see how close we almost came to getting busted? I don't know about you, but I'm not trying to get kicked out of school for hazing."

"I agree," Raquelle added, stepping up next to Lynn. "This is enough for tonight." She turned to us. "We'll see you guys tomorrow."

I was actually relieved and said a mental thank-you to Mr. Washington. Jasmine was on the edge. I could tell she was still upset. I was about to say something to her as we walked back to Alexis's car, but she glared at me.

"Don't. Don't say one word to me." She climbed in the backseat, closed her eyes, and didn't say a thing for the rest of the ride home.

6

Camille

We hadn't even been accepted into the Theta Ladies yet, but they were still making us do things that I knew we had no business doing, especially after the advisor gave us that whole "no hazing" speech. After last night, especially, I would have thought they'd take it a little easier. But it seemed like things had only gotten worse.

"Camille, be a doll and go run get me a Coke," Tori said. Me, Angel, Tameka, Jasmine, and two other girls who were interested in the Thetas were sitting at the back cafeteria table with several members. I had to promise to pay for Jasmine's lunch for the next two weeks just to get her to agree to sit and have lunch with us.

"Sure," I said, standing up. I didn't mind playing the fetch-it girl. I knew it was all part of the process. The members got to order around the girls who were interested. I'd read up on hazing on the Internet, and knew it was totally illegal, but to me, that was the fun part of it all. Well, except for the running and push-ups.

I made my way over to the soda machine and reached in my jeans pocket to fish out a dollar—since of course Tori didn't give me any money. I got the soda and sprinted back over to the table.

"Here you go." I handed the soda to Tori.

She frowned up at it. "Oh, no. I said a Diet Coke."

I looked confused. "I could've sworn you said Coke."

Jasmine, who had started eating her pizza, looked at Tori, then at me. "She *did* say Coke."

Tori turned up her nose as she looked at Jasmine, then at the Coke can that sat in front of her. "Look, I know what I said. Some people may not care how regular Coke makes them blow up like an Amazon, but *I* do," she stressed.

I cringed because if it was one thing I knew Jasmine couldn't stand, it was somebody talking about her size. Even though she'd lost some weight, she was still the biggest of all of us.

"It's no biggie. I can run get a Diet Coke," I quickly said, silently pleading with Jasmine not to go off.

"No, I want Miss-I-got-something-to-say-even-though-nobody-is-talking-to-me to go get me something to drink," Tori said, cutting her eyes at Jasmine.

Jasmine threw her half-eaten pizza down on her plate and sat up straighter. She was so about to lose it.

"Really, I don't mind," I interjected.

"Camille, have a seat," Tori said, her voice getting forceful. "Jasmine, go get me a Diet Coke. Now!"

Angel closed her eyes like she was praying for Jasmine not to go off as well. Tameka sat with her eyes wide like she couldn't believe Jasmine wasn't up and moving. I slid down in my seat as Jasmine bit down on her bottom lip. I was overjoyed when she finally smiled and stood. "Fine. I'll go get you a Diet Coke." She held out her hand toward Tori. "I'll need one dollar."

Tori groaned in disgust but dug in her purse and pulled out four quarters. She dropped the money in Jasmine's hand. I could tell it took everything in Jasmine's power not to fling the money upside Tori's head.

Tori rolled her eyes as soon as Jasmine walked off. She leaned in and whispered something to Alisha, the girl sitting next to her, and they both busted out laughing.

I took a bite of my food in silence. We still had two days before they made a decision on us, so I was really hoping Jasmine could keep her cool until then.

"Here's your Diet Coke," Jasmine said as she approached the table.

"Can you pop the top, please?" Tori casually said, as she turned back to Alisha like she was in a deep conversation.

Jasmine took a deep breath, then popped the top and sat the soda down in front of Tori.

Tori didn't bother to look at Jasmine as she continued her conversation with Alisha, this time talking real loud.

"So anyway, as I was saying, Donovan will be here this weekend and he can't stop talking about all the special things he has planned for us."

I don't think I'd ever been so anxious for the bell to ring and for lunch to be over!

Tori had done everything under the sun to get Donovan to be with her when him and Jasmine were going together.

After Donovan left for college, him and Jasmine broke up, but it was obvious she still loved him. So to hear Tori talking about him, I just knew would set her off.

". . . And he wants me to come up to watch him play," Tori continued.

I was just about to try and start up a conversation with Jasmine about something, anything, when Tori turned to her.

"You know, I just thought about it—didn't you mess with Donovan for a minute?" she asked.

I hung my head. Tori knew doggone well that what Donovan and Jasmine had was more than just "messing around." And it was definitely longer than "a minute."

She looked at Jasmine innocently, like she was waiting on her to respond. Jasmine just continued biting her bottom lip. Tori shrugged and turned back to Alisha. "Guess the cat has her tongue. Oh well, anyway, wait until you see the dress I'm wearing for our date this weekend. Baby, those college girls won't have anything on me. I know when

Donovan sees me in that dress, he won't be able to keep his hands off of me."

I guess Jasmine had heard all she could stomach because she grabbed her soda and her plate and got up from the table. Tori and Alisha laughed as she stomped off.

"Ooooh, you'd better go see about your little friend. She looks mad as all get-out," Alisha said to me.

"*Little?* As big as she is? Please," Tori said and they both cracked up laughing again.

"Yeah, I need to get to class anyway," I said, getting up from the table as well. Angel followed me. It didn't surprise me that Tameka kept her seat.

We caught up with Jasmine just outside the cafeteria. She was fuming.

I walked up to her, poised to begin my speech.

She held up her hand and stopped me before I could say a word. "Camille, leave me alone. I swear, I'm two seconds from punching something. Or somebody."

"Why are you letting her get to you?" I asked.

"Yeah," Angel chimed in. "You know they just mess with us to get under our skin. That's what they're supposed to do to girls trying to join."

"Well, that's stupid," Jasmine snapped. "Why would they want to make me mad on purpose?"

I shrugged. "It's just all part of the process."

"Well, it's a stupid process."

Just then the bell rang and everyone began filing out of

the lunchroom. We were about to head to our classes when we heard Tori calling me.

"Oh, Camille," she said, catching up to us and handing me a piece of paper. "Can you go turn in my history essay to Mrs. King? It's due by fifth period."

Okay, I was getting tired of her, too. Still, I took the paper.

"Thanks, girl," Tori said, without giving me time to respond. She stepped around me and immediately bumped into Jasmine. Tori's backpack fell open and all of her books came tumbling out. I couldn't be sure, but it almost seemed like Tori had done it on purpose.

"Dang! Would your big behind watch where you're going? Good grief!" Tori said, loud enough to make several people passing by stop and start staring. "Pick my stuff up!" She demanded. "You're going to make me late for class!"

Jasmine didn't respond. She just stood looking at Tori like she was crazy.

"Is all that fat clogging your ears?" Tori snapped. Several people standing around started "ooohing" and "aahing."

Angel immediately started picking up the books.

"I don't want you to get it," Tori snapped at her. "I want her to get it. She knocked the books out so she needs to pick them up." Tori pushed Jasmine's shoulder. "And hurry up because I don't have all day."

I saw the fire in Jasmine's eyes and knew it was all over.

"Get your own books," Jasmine hissed. "And if you ever

put your stank hands on me again I will break your freakin' arm."

"Hit her in the mouth!" some stupid boy yelled.

Tori seemed surprised for a minute, but quickly regained her confidence as she stepped closer toward Jasmine. "Umph, I don't know what Donovan ever saw in your big, food-stamp-carrying, ghetto tomboy behind."

Jasmine's chest heaved up and down as she glared at her. She was from the hood and even though her mother was a hard worker, her family was still on welfare. So Jasmine was real sensitive about her background.

"What, you gonna hit me now?" Tori said, cocking her head. "I happen to know that you had to transfer to Madison in the first place because you got kicked out of your other school for fighting. One more fight and you're expelled from the district for good." She smiled as she stepped closer. "So go ahead, take your best shot."

Jasmine clenched her fists. "Touch me again and see how much I care about getting kicked out of school."

"Come on, Jasmine, chill," Angel whispered as she lightly touched Jasmine's arm.

Jasmine jerked her arm away but kept her glare on Tori.

"Yeah, Jasmine, *chill*," Tori said. "Or you can forget about ever being a Theta."

Jasmine took a deep breath, calming herself. "It's already forgotten. Because I don't want or need your little funky sorority."

Tori sucked her teeth. "Oh, we weren't funky when you were all up in our face trying to be a member."

"I ain't never been all up in your face."

"Well, what did you apply for then?" Tori said.

"Call it temporary insanity, peer pressure, whatever. But consider this my withdrawal notice." Jasmine reached over and snatched Tori's history essay from me. She held it up, then ripped it in half. "You're lucky your paper is all that I'm tearing up." She flung the torn paper in Tori's face before turning and walking off.

My mouth—as well as Tori's—fell open in shock. But Jasmine couldn't care less as she strutted down the hall to her next class.

7

Jasmine

They got it twisted if they thought I was just gonna sit there and take Tori's mess!

I didn't need to be a part of *nothing* that bad. I knew Camille was going to try and come give me some lame excuse about why I should give the Thetas another chance. And I was right because she, Angel, and Tameka were waiting at my locker after my last class.

"Camille, don't even start with me because I'm not trying to hear you," I said as I opened my locker and stuffed my English book in.

"Come on, Jasmine. Why are you trippin'?" Tameka asked.

I slammed the locker shut. "You need to ask that snob Tori why she's trippin'."

"They really are nice girls," Tameka said.

I turned and stared at her. "Do your lips hurt?"

She looked confused. "My lips? Why?"

"I'm just wondering if your lips are sore from playing kiss-up."

Tameka rolled her eyes, but I didn't care. I was too through. "Look, you guys might be okay with running around like a slave or something, but I'm not with that," I told them.

Camille tried to convince me with, "Jasmine, you know this is all a big game."

"Game over." I headed down the hall and out the building. Camille, of course, was on my heels and Angel and Tameka were right behind her.

"Jaz, it's just all part of what they do," Tameka said as they caught up with me.

"Yeah, it's all in fun," Camille added.

Tameka, I wasn't even trying to hear. As for Camille, she was my girl and all, but she was definitely losing her mind. I spun on her. "Camille, there was nothing fun about today. There was nothing fun about last night. There is nothing fun at all about being humiliated, degraded, and talked to like you're crazy. If that's what gets you off, then fine. But as for me, no thanks."

"It's not that bad," Angel chimed in.

I turned to her and shook my head. "Angel, I can't believe you're falling for this mess. Half the time, they act like you're not even there. I don't understand why you even want to be a part of this."

Camille let out a long sigh. "You're judging the whole

organization by one person. It's not even like that. Tori is just one person in the group."

"She seems to be the only one that matters since everybody else is too scared to speak out against her." It was my turn to let out a frustrated sigh. They were making my head hurt. "Look, I told y'all. I'm out. You can stay and take that crap all you want, but I'm done. The bad part is, you guys are taking all of this mess and you don't even know if you've been accepted."

"We're supposed to get our letters Friday." Camille pouted. "But Raquelle told me she thinks we're a shoo-in."

"Whatever, Camille." I was about to add something else when I looked up and saw Tori and her crew heading our way. I swear, if she said something out of line to me, I was gon' haul off and knock her in her jaw. That's why I decided it would be best if I bounced.

"I'm gone. I'll see you guys later. Have fun getting treated like dirt."

I left before they could say another word. More power to them. But just like I tried to tell them from jump, I'm not cut out to be a sorority girl.

8

Camille

Today was a bittersweet day. One on hand, I was happy because we were supposed to be getting our letters of acceptance delivered to our lockers today after school. On the other, I was upset because I really wished Jasmine was going through the process with us. But after Jasmine went off on Tori the day before yesterday, I knew there was no way in the world that would happen.

Even still, me, Tameka, Angel, and Alexis were so excited. We'd all agreed to get our letters then meet behind the bleachers at the track after school and open them together. Alexis had skipped out of her last class early so she could come pick up her letter from the Theta advisor.

"I sure wish Jasmine was here," Angel said as we pulled out our letters.

I sighed. "I know. Me, too."

"You don't think our friendship will suffer behind all of this, do you?" Alexis asked.

"Nah," I replied, hoping that I wasn't just trying to be optimistic. Jasmine had missed school yesterday and today because she was sick and she hadn't been in a talkative mood when I called her. I could tell she was still upset so I just left her alone. "She's just mad at Tori right now. I think she'll be fine with us when she gets over that."

We all stood in silence for a moment, but the excitement began to overtake us.

"Okay, let's open the letters," Tameka finally said.

"Wait," I excitedly said before anyone could get their letters open. "Are we going to open them all together or one at a time?"

"All together," Angel responded.

Tameka and Alexis nodded in agreement.

"On the count of three," I said, holding up my envelope. "One, two, *three*!"

We all tore open our envelopes. My eyes immediately zoomed in on the word "congratulations." I started squealing as I jumped up and down. Alexis and Tameka were doing the same.

"I'm in!" Tameka shouted.

"Me, too!" I sang.

"Me, three," Alexis echoed.

I high-fived Alexis. "As if we had any doubts."

We waited for Angel to start screaming as well, but she stood quietly, the letter gripped firmly in her hand.

"Come on, slowpoke," I said. "Hurry up so we can go celebrate."

Angel looked up, her eyes filling with tears. "It looks like you guys will have to celebrate without me. I didn't make it," she said softly.

The smiles left our faces. "What?" Alexis and I said at the same time.

"You heard me. I got rejected." Angel balled the letter up and stuffed it down in her book bag.

"You're kidding, right?" I said, reaching in her bag and grabbing the letter.

"I wouldn't kid about something like this." Her voice was shaky.

I quickly scanned the letter. The words "sorry" and "try again next year" seemed to be blaring across the page.

I was speechless. It never crossed my mind that any of us might get rejected. And definitely not sweet, quiet Angel.

"I don't understand," Alexis said. "How can they reject you? You're the nicest one of us all."

Angel shrugged, trying to fight back tears. "I guess they just didn't like me." She took a deep breath. "But don't worry about it. You guys got in. That's all that really matters."

"No, it's not," I said. "We were *all* supposed to get in."

"Well, we all didn't," Angel replied matter-of-factly as she threw her book bag over her shoulder. "It's probably for the best anyway. I need to be focused on school and raising Angelica."

I could tell she didn't mean that and was just trying to say something to ease the pain.

"D-do you think they rejected you because you have a baby?" Tameka said.

"I don't know," Angel responded. "Maybe. Probably. Who knows? Look, it's no big deal. You all go on and celebrate. You know everybody is going to be gathered in the courtyard after school."

We were supposed to keep everything a secret, but some of the girls had already said they were going to hang out after school in the courtyard if they made it into the Theta Ladies.

"Angel . . ." My voice trailed off. I didn't know what to say.

Angel forced a smile. "Really, Camille, I'm fine. You guys go have fun." She looked at her watch. "I gotta go or I'll miss the bus. Call me later."

We stood speechless as Angel darted off. And I didn't know whether to turn flips of joy or break out in tears.

9

Camille

"So, I guess you guys are happy now?" Jasmine said as she walked into tonight's Good Girlz meeting. "You made it into your precious little sorority."

"How'd you know?" Alexis asked.

"I saw Angel on the way home. She was pretty bummed out. But I'm sure you don't care."

"Jasmine, don't start," I moaned.

Me, Alexis, and Tameka had hung out with a bunch of other girls that had gotten invitations from the Thetas. Seven of the nine girls that were at the park with us had made it in. They'd all gone out to eat, but me and Alexis decided to go to the Good Girlz meeting. We would've skipped it, but we didn't want Miss Rachel trippin'. Besides, I think both of us wanted to check on Angel.

Tameka didn't seem bothered about Angel or missing the meeting, though. I don't know if she thought Rachel wouldn't do anything to her because that was her aunt or if she just didn't care. She just went with the other new Thetas.

"No, seriously, that's all that matters to you guys—that you're now Thetas." Jasmine plopped down in the chair next to me.

"We're not Thetas yet," Alexis pointed out. "We just got letters of invitation. We still have to go through a process before we get in."

"Get into what?" Rachel asked as she walked into the room.

"Camille, Tameka, and Alexis made it into their little sorority." Jasmine smirked.

"Well, congratulations." She smiled, then looked around. "Wait a minute. You said Camille, Tameka, and Alexis. Does that mean Angel didn't make it?" Of course, we had filled Miss Rachel in on the fact that we were all trying to be Thetas in the first place.

"Answer me, somebody," Rachel said. "Does that mean Angel didn't make it?"

Neither me nor Alexis said anything.

"That's exactly what it means," Jasmine replied, shaking her head. "Which probably explains why she isn't here now. I saw her on the way home, and although she tried to act like she was fine, I know she wasn't. And you know she must be upset because Angel never misses a meeting."

A worried look crossed Rachel's face. "Oh, I hate to hear that. Maybe I should give her a call."

Jasmine sucked her teeth and shot us disgusted looks. "Well, personally, I think Camille, Tameka, and Alexis should tell the Thetas what they can do with their little acceptance letter," she said.

Alexis's mouth dropped open. "That's crazy. Why should we not accept it just because Angel didn't make it?" she asked.

Jasmine rolled her eyes. "That's just like you to be so selfish. How about thinking about someone else for a change?"

"What's that supposed to mean?" Alexis snapped. "I know you're not talking about me being selfish. Not when you're always borrowing my stuff."

Jasmine sat up in her seat and pointed at Alexis. "Look, don't be throwing stuff up in my face. I can't stand when somebody does something for me then throws it up in my face."

"Girls, calm down, please," Rachel interjected.

Jasmine crossed her arms across her chest and leaned back in her seat. "I don't know what you guys are getting all excited for anyway. You act like this is a real college sorority or something," she mumbled.

"Are you sure that Angel is upset?" Rachel asked.

"Like I said, the fact that she isn't here says it all," Jasmine barked.

Rachel ran her fingers through her hair, then turned to me. "Have you talked to Angel? Is she okay?"

I shrugged. "When we got our letters, she said she was cool. She wants us to go ahead and accept the invitation." I knew Angel was upset but I was hoping she really meant it when she said that.

"Well, if Angel doesn't have a problem with them being Thetas, I don't see why you do, Jasmine," Rachel said.

Jasmine threw up her hands. "Like Angel would really say something if she did have a problem with it. The bottom line is the Thetas didn't think Angel, the nicest person on the face of the planet, was good enough for their little sorority, so I think all of them should tell the Thetas what they can do with their little invitations. But that's just my two cents."

"Jasmine is just being her usual foul self," Alexis said, shaking her head.

"Whatever," Jasmine mumbled.

"Well, I just hope you all stay friends and don't let this sorority stuff mess that up," Rachel said. She took her seat at the front of the room. "And as a matter of fact, that's what I wanted to talk to you girls about today, what makes a friend."

Miss Rachel spent the next thirty minutes talking to us about true friendship. As she usually does, she even incorporated a few Bible verses to hammer home her point.

"I want you all to take a look at Proverbs 12:26 when you get a chance," Rachel said, flipping through the Bible. "It basically says that the righteous should choose his friends carefully for the way of the wicked leads them astray."

"Are you saying the Theta Ladies are wicked?" I asked, not sure where she was going.

"No," Rachel shook her head. "That verse is specifically telling us that if we do not choose our friends very carefully in this life, we could end up choosing the wrong type of people to become friends with and they can then end up leading us astray from God and with what He wants to do with our lives. So for that reason I want you to be careful in choosing your friends. You girls have a true friendship here. Don't let outside forces threaten that and remember that in order to have a friend, you must be a friend." She looked us in the eye one by one. "I want each of you to ask yourself if you are being a true friend."

I thought about that for a minute. I *was* being a friend. Jasmine was the one that was trippin'.

Miss Rachel finally began wrapping up the meeting, and made us promise to call Angel.

"Miss Rachel, did you ever think of joining a sorority?" Alexis asked, as we started gathering up our stuff to leave. I was hoping that we'd left that topic alone, but Alexis seemed oblivious to the tensions it was creating.

Rachel smiled. "Well, I didn't go to college, and we didn't have sororities when I was in high school. But if they did, I probably wouldn't have joined. Sororities were never my cup of tea."

"That's what I'm talking about," Jasmine said.

"But my mother was in a sorority and she loved it," Rachel added. "She was active until the day she died."

"My mom is in one, too," I added. "But she works so much she's not able to go to meetings and stuff. I do remember all the good times she said she had in college, though."

"Operative word—college," Jasmine interjected. "They probably weren't stupid enough to make people do stuff like push-ups and being somebody's slaves."

Rachel jumped in before we could get started arguing again. "The bottom line is you have to remember this is different. It's high school. So, technically, it's not a bona fide sorority."

Jasmine twisted up her lips. "Somebody better tell the Thetas that because they sure think they are."

I was about to protest some more, but Jasmine grabbed her backpack and headed to the door.

"I'm tired of talkin' about this. Y'all got your wish, so everything's everything," she said. "Anyway, I'm out. My chickenhead brother should be outside."

"Ooooh, tell Jaquan I said hi," Alexis said, her eyes lighting up.

Jasmine rolled her eyes. "Yeah, right."

Alexis and Jaquan, Jasmine's fifteen-year-old brother, had dated for a couple of weeks last year—against Jasmine's advice. And when he played her, like Jasmine said he does all of his girlfriends, she got mad at Jasmine. But they eventually worked out their differences. Alexis still flirted with Jaquan from time to time, though.

"You're just upset because you wanted me to be your sister-in-law," Alexis called out after her.

Jasmine waved her off. "Whatever, girl." She laughed. "In your dreams. I'll see you guys later."

I was actually glad the subject had switched to Jaquan. I knew no matter what I said, we'd never see eye-to-eye when it came to the Thetas. And the fact that we were able to go from arguing about that to laughing and joking again proved to me that our friendship was strong enough to overcome anything—even Angel's rejection from the Thetas.

10

Camille

I so did not want to go into the cafeteria. But as I looked over at Alisha, giggling like a little girl as she pointed at my outfit, I knew I didn't have much choice. Luckily, I wasn't the only one looking crazy. The six girls behind me were jacked up, too.

"Okay, ladies, let's go," Alisha sang.

A few of us let out groans as we marched toward the cafeteria. Only Tameka seemed like she wasn't fazed in the least bit about dressing like some 1970s rejects.

Sure, me and Alexis were into the whole Theta thing, but Tameka had taken it to a whole new level. We'd only been pledging three days, but she was always brownnosing with the Thetas, trying to get on their good side. And she did anything they asked—no matter how stupid—with a big smile on her face.

As instructed, we went our separate ways as we passed the teachers' lounge by the cafeteria. School officials considered it hazing when you made someone dress up against their will. So we'd been told to act normally and say we just felt like dressing silly if a teacher approached us. Of course, the teachers weren't stupid. They knew the real deal, but most of them just blew it off, as long as it didn't get too out of hand.

I made my way over to the soda machine while I looked around for Jasmine and Angel, since we always ate lunch together. I hadn't seen Angel during first period, so maybe she wasn't even at school, I thought. I felt a little guilty as I found myself hoping she wasn't here because I really didn't know what to say to her. I hadn't seen her since we got our letters, and she wasn't returning any of my phone calls.

I hated to tell Jasmine, but the Thetas had said that we had to eat with them today and every day during our pledge week.

"Eeewwww, who dressed you this morning? Stevie Wonder?"

I hadn't even noticed Jasmine come up behind me. She ran her eyes up and down the bright yellow-and-black polka dot shirt and pink pinstriped pants I was wearing. The pants legs were tucked into white tube socks.

"Shut up! I had no choice," I said.

She turned her nose up. "For real, though. What's with the get-up?"

I sighed. Although Jasmine didn't cut for the Thetas, I knew she'd never tell on us, so I told her the truth.

"The Thetas are making us wear these crazy outfits." I sulked as I noticed people pointing at me and giggling under their breath. I didn't know how much more of this I would be able to take. This whole pledging thing was truly over-rated. Yesterday, we had to eat some raw eggs. The day before that, we had to walk around school barefoot. Luckily, Mr. Washington quickly nipped that in the bud. Plus, I didn't think it was fair that Alexis got out of being humiliated at school. I wished I went to a different school.

Jasmine shook her head at me in disgust. "I can't believe you are letting those girls punk you like that. Do you see them coming to school dressed like idiots?"

Before I could respond, two of the girls pledging with me walked by in similar outfits. Jasmine laughed. "Y'all look like the three blind mice. I might have to find some-one else to eat lunch with. Even I don't want to be seen with you dressed like that. You're killing my rep," she joked.

I couldn't help but laugh. "You don't have a rep." I looked at my outfit. "But you're right. I wouldn't want to be seen with me either."

"Maybe I should catch up with you later." She took another glance at my outfit and shook her head. "Make that tomorrow. Unless of course they make y'all wear dia-pers or something." She laughed. "Naw, I'm just messin' with you. If it doesn't bother you, it doesn't bother me. Are we sitting outside today?" She motioned toward the patio door.

"Ummmm, I know you really don't want to be around me, girl. And it . . . it's cool," I stammered. "I have to sit with my pledge sisters anyway."

Jasmine looked at me like her feelings were really hurt. She was about to say something, but apparently changed her mind because she shook her head and mumbled something about it not even being worth it as she turned and walked away. I felt bad about sticking Jasmine out like that. The Thetas had let us sit where we wanted the first few days, but then had made it clear that we all had to start sitting together today. I'm sure that was so they could torture us some more. I got my lunch and went and sat down next to Kim, one of my pledge sisters.

I didn't see Tori at the table in front of me—until I heard her say loudly, "I know you see me. Don't you have something to say to me?"

I took a deep breath before getting up and going to stand directly in front of Tori. I put on my fakest smile and repeated the daily greeting we were required to say every time we saw one of the Thetas: "Greetings, Big Sister Beautiful One. I humbly greet you this beautiful day with much respect and gratitude toward you for allowing me the opportunity to serve you. What can I do to make your day better?"

"Nothing right now, pledge. You are dismissed. Besides, you're blocking my view," she said as she tried to look around me. I turned to go back to my seat and saw Kalvin, one of the cutest boys in school and captain of the football team. He was standing a few tables away, laughing with some of his teammates. This boy was superfine and word around school was that he didn't have a girlfriend. He and I had sixth period Spanish together. I'd had my eye on him for a couple of months and we had even flirted with each other a couple of times. It had never gone anywhere, though. But I was hoping that one day it would. That's why there was no way I was going to let him see me looking like this. I quickly and quietly tried to ease back to my seat unnoticed.

"Camille," Tori called just as I was about to sit down. "Get over here now!"

I walked back over to her, dreading what she had in store this time.

"We've been discussing something and we need you to help us get the answer. I need you to go over and ask Kalvin if he wears boxers or briefs. And oh yeah, ask him if you can borrow a pair."

My mouth dropped. Had she lost her mind? I thought about telling all of them what they could do for me, but I remembered how bad I wanted this. I would just have to explain to Kalvin later the reason for my appearance. Maybe he wouldn't be too turned off by this outfit.

I slowly walked up to the football players and stood behind Kalvin. He was so engrossed in their conversation that, at first, he didn't even see me standing there. One of his buddies looked up, smiled, and then nudged Kalvin.

"Oh, hey Camille," Kalvin said with a confused look on his face. All of his friends had the same expression.

My face was beet red at this point. I almost turned around and took off running. I looked at my feet and asked quietly, "Umm, do you wear boxers or briefs?"

"What?"

"Do you wear boxers or briefs?" I repeated, this time with more force. I looked at the guys behind him. All of them were cracking up laughing.

One of them said, "Yeah, dog, which one is it—boxers or briefs?"

Kalvin smiled like he finally understood. "Boxers, why?"

"Can a sista borrow a pair?"

"Sure, you want the ones I got on now?" he joked.

I shook my head no. "Maybe you can just bring me a pair tomorrow." I didn't know if I was supposed to get a fresh pair or what, but at that point, it didn't matter. I was so embarrassed, I just wanted to get away.

"I guess I can do that for you. Whatchu gon' do for me?" He licked his lips. Any other time I would have found that to be sexy and I would've flirted back. But considering how I was looking, I was so not in a flirtatious mood.

"How 'bout I just do your Spanish homework?"

"That's really not what I had in mind." He stepped closer to me.

I put up a hand to stop him. "I can do the homework.

That's it." As bad as I wanted to get with him, I definitely didn't want him thinking I was easy.

He moved back and laughed. "I guess that'll have to do. For now."

"Thank you." I glanced over at Tori, who was no longer smiling. It was obvious she hadn't intended on Kalvin trying to flirt with me. "Well, I better get going."

Before I could say anything, he leaned over and kissed me on the cheek. "Keep your head up. Don't let them get to you," he whispered. "And maybe after this is all over, we can hook up."

He actually seemed genuine, and Lord knows I'd love to hook up with his fine behind.

"That sounds good to me."

Kalvin had never paid me much attention, probably because some girl was always up in his face. So I was happily surprised about him trying to talk to me.

"I gotta go," I hurriedly said. "Thanks for the boxers. I'll get them from you tomorrow." I paused. "And I'll give you my number in sixth period." I flashed a big smile before I took off.

I never would've had the courage to approach Kalvin on my own, so if we did hook up, maybe one good thing would come out of the pledge mess after all.

11

Jasmine

"So you gave up on the Thetas?"

I turned to see C. J. standing against my locker, his signature smile making my heart flutter against my will. I totally did not understand why I was feeling the way I was now. I didn't like C. J. At least not in that way, I tried to tell myself. But it's like my heart was taking over or something because I found myself smiling back.

"Naw. That's not for me," I said, trying to maintain my hard composure.

"I didn't think it was."

"But I thought you said I'd make a good Theta."

"I did say that. And I still think you would, but I just didn't see you going through with it, you know, taking all that stuff they dish out."

"I guess you knew me better than I knew myself." I laughed as I closed my locker door.

He flashed that sexy grin at me.

"What?" I asked, clutching my history book closer. I didn't like him staring at me like that. Camille is the boy-crazy one in our group. Yeah, I fell head over heels for Donovan, but for the most part, I wasn't trying to get wrapped up in no dude. Shoot, I'd done that with Donovan and look what happened. He dumped me as soon as he got to college.

"What?" I repeated. "Why are you standing there grinning at me, looking all stupid?"

"Because you have a gorgeous smile. And you never let me see you smile. You're always frowned up, like you're ready to jump somebody or something."

"Boy, what do you want?" I rolled my eyes as I continued to fight back my smile. I didn't want him to think he was getting to me.

"I keep telling you I want you." He moved closer to me. "I want you to be my girl."

My eyes grew wide. C. J. flirted with me all the time, but he had never laid it out on the table like that. "Boy, please," I managed to say after I gathered my composure. I stepped around him and headed toward the double doors that led out to the front of the school. I was hooking up with Camille and Alexis to head straight to our Good Girlz meeting. We'd tried to see if Angel wanted to catch a ride but she still wasn't talking to any of us. Although I couldn't for the life of me understand why she was mad at me. And Tameka was nowhere to be found. She probably was off shining Tori's shoes.

"I'm serious," C. J. said, running to catch up with me. "We've been playing games since we first met."

"You might've been playing games, but I wasn't." I kept marching across the grassy area at the front of the campus. I don't know why I couldn't stop and hear him out because quiet as it was kept, I was really starting to feel him.

C. J. grabbed my arm and stopped me. "We both were playing games."

I snatched my arm away. "Really, *we* weren't. Or at least I wasn't. I *really* didn't like you. You were a jerk with a capital J."

C. J. smiled and held up one finger. "Aha!"

"Aha what?"

"You said, '*didn't* like you.' As in past tense." He stepped closer to me again. I could smell his Cool Water cologne. I loved Cool Water. My brother wore it all the time. Only his didn't smell as good as C. J.'s because he was always putting on too much.

"So, tell the truth, Jasmine." He gently ran his hand down the side of my cheek. "You like me now."

I swear to God, I wanted to jerk away from him. Turn up my lips, roll my eyes, suck my teeth, anything to let him know he was crazy. But it was like my brain wasn't sending the message to my body. In fact, I actually felt goose bumps popping up.

C. J. didn't give me time to shake myself out of my trance. He leaned in and kissed me lightly on the mouth, letting his tongue peek out just a little bit to dance around the edge of my lips.

He leaned back and licked his lips. "Mmm, cherry lip gloss. My favorite." He stared into my eyes, like he was looking through to my soul. Dang! I took a deep breath. That so sounded like some sappy mess Camille would say.

C. J. took my hand. "Jasmine, I know I was a jerk, with a capital J," he said with a smile. "But that's because I was a boy who didn't know how to let you know I thought you were so fine. But I'm a man now. And I am totally feeling you. And I'm stepping to you the right way." He paused. "You think about that. I want you to be my girl. And I'm not gon' rest until I have you."

He leaned in and quickly kissed me on the lips again, before dropping my hand. He pulled out a folded-up piece of paper, then pushed it down in my jeans pocket. "Here's my number. Call me." He walked off before I could will my vocal cords to work again.

"Oh. My. God!"

Alexis' voice startled me out of my trance. She and Camille were standing right behind me. I hadn't even noticed them walk up. Both of their mouths were wide open.

"That was some Rico Suave stuff!" Camille gasped.

I shook my head, finally coming to my senses. "Whatever," I replied. I definitely was not about to let them see me swooning over C. J. of all people.

"Was that nerdy C. J.?" Camille asked.

Alexis leaned to the side and watched C. J. get into his souped-up black Toyota Camry. "Girl, ain't nothing nerdy about that boy. He is too cute."

"I know," Camille echoed. "It's like he grew into a totally different person over the summer. He used to be scrawny and nerdy. I mean, he ain't all buff or nothing; he's that skinny sort of fine."

"Mmm-mmm, like solid. And girl, that pretty chocolate skin. Lord Jesus, help me." Alexis laughed as she gave Camille a high five.

I don't know why, but I felt a tinge of jealousy. "Would you all stop talking about him like he's a T-bone steak or something."

Alexis giggled. "Sounds like somebody's jealous," she sang.

"Whatever. I don't want that boy." I turned and marched toward the parking lot. "Alexis, where'd you park?"

Camille and Alexis quickly followed me, laughing. "Jasmine and C. J. sittin' in a tree. K-i-s-s-i-n-g," Camille sang.

I stopped and turned to them. "Oh my God. Would you grow up?" I told Camille.

Alexis draped her arm through Camille's and joined in, singing, "First comes love, then comes marriage. Then comes Jasmine with a baby carriage."

I rolled my eyes, turned, and continued walking. "You guys are so first grade."

They both caught up and walked on either side of me. "Okay, okay. We're just being silly," Alexis said.

"But tell the truth." Camille jumped in front of me. "You like him, don't you?"

I stopped before I ran right into her. I contemplated telling them no, but then I thought, why was I lying about it? I was almost grown. These were my girls. If I couldn't tell them how I was feeling, I couldn't tell anyone.

"Okay, okay," I said, breaking out in a huge smile. "He is cute, isn't he?"

They squealed, dancing around like I had just said I was going on a date with Ne-Yo or something.

"What's the big deal?" I asked.

"You, finally admitting what we've known all along," Camille replied.

"And that is?"

"That you're feeling C. J.," Camille said matter-of-factly. She put her hands on her hips. "So, what are you going to do about it?"

I hadn't thought that far. "Nothing," I said. "I mean, there's really nothing going on with us."

"That kiss wasn't nothing," Alexis said.

"For real," Camille added. "Y'all making out in public like you some hoochie mama," she joked.

"We were not making out," I protested. "He just kissed me." I smiled again, recalling the way C. J.'s lips felt against mine. "He did say he wanted me to be his girl, though."

Camille raised her eyebrows like she was waiting on me to continue. "And you told him yes, right?"

"I didn't tell him anything."

"Well, you're going to call him when you get home and tell him yes, right?" Alexis prodded.

I thought about it for a minute. "Maybe I will. Maybe I won't."

"Girl, you'd better call that boy," Camille said. "I saw him give you his number."

"Okay, Inspector Gadget. How do you know what was on the paper?"

"What else would he be stuffing in your pants?" Alexis replied.

"Unless he was just trying to cop a feel," Camille added.

I threw up my hands as I started back toward the parking lot. "What? Are you guys spying on me or something?"

"We weren't spying. We were coming to meet you and just stayed back to give you some privacy," Camille said, trying to sound all innocent.

I tsked. "Mmm-hmmm, stayed back just far enough to be able to hear."

"Well, of course," they replied in unison.

We all busted out laughing. I was surprised because I was feeling better than I had in a long time. I was chillin' with my best friends and, from the looks of things, headed toward a new love. Life couldn't really get any better than that.

12

Camille

I took in every inch of Kalvin. He was so fine, it wasn't even funny. His hair was braided back into tight zigzag braids. He wore Sean John jeans, a bright yellow Sean John T-shirt, and the newest Jordans.

I'd been through my share of boyfriends, but if I could make Kalvin mine, he'd top any other guy I'd ever dated.

"Here's your Spanish homework." I smiled as I handed Kalvin the paper. I'd spent all last night making sure it was perfectly done. I'd purposely missed two questions so the teacher wouldn't get suspicious, but the rest of it I was sure would garner him an A.

"And here are my boxers." He held them up with both hands.

"Oh my God." I quickly grabbed them and stuffed them down in my bag as I looked around nervously. The fact that I had to ask for them in the first place was embarrassing enough. I didn't need him flashing them right there in the hallway for the whole world to see.

"What? You're afraid someone might see you collecting boys' boxers?" Kalvin laughed.

"Please, it's bad enough I have to do this silly stuff." I shook my head as I zipped up my bag. One girl had already seen them and was looking at me crazy. I shot her a look that told her to mind her own business.

"Oh, it's no big deal. Everybody knows it's all part of your pledging," Kalvin said.

I sighed. "Everyone's not supposed to know about our pledging."

"Well, they do." Kalvin lifted his left hand to move a strand of hair away from my face. "So, tell me, why does a pretty girl like you want to be a Theta Lady anyway?"

"I just do." As cute as he was, his gaze was starting to make me uncomfortable. He looked like he wanted to tear my clothes off right then and there, and I didn't like that.

"I'm sure you gave a better answer than 'I just do' when they asked."

He was now running his hand up and down my arm. I kind of eased away from his touch. "I just like what the Thetas are about," I said.

"So do they make you get with guys or anything like that?" he asked. His voice was husky as he looked me dead in the eye.

"Excuse me?" I cocked my head. "What did you just say?"

"You heard me." The smile was gone from his face now and he looked serious as a heart attack. "I mean, they got you approaching guys for their underwear and all. I'm just wondering what else they have you doing. Or *who* they have you doing."

I know I was feeling Kalvin and all, but I surely didn't want him thinking this was that kind of party. I didn't try hiding my frown.

"They don't have us *doing* anyone. We just do stupid tasks, but nothing like that," I snapped.

"Well, I heard some pretty wild stories."

"Well, you heard wrong."

"Dang, baby, chill," he said, holding up his hands like he was surrendering. "But I sure do hate that the rumors aren't true." He moved in closer to me. I put up my hand to hold him off.

"Wait a minute. You need to slow your roll. I don't know what you're thinking, but I'm not even like that."

Kalvin backed up and laughed. "Whatever you say."

I didn't know if he was being sarcastic or what, but our Spanish teacher appeared in the doorway, motioning for us to go into the classroom.

Kalvin walked ahead of me, bouncing to his seat at the back of the classroom. Suddenly, he wasn't as cute as he was before.

I let out a disgusted sigh as I followed him into the

classroom. I knew Tori had a bad reputation, although I didn't know how much of it was true. But now Kalvin had me wondering. On top of everything else, did I have to be concerned with messing up my name just because I wanted to be a Theta?

13

Camille

I was so sick of doing stupid stuff, I didn't know what to do. It had been a whole week of dressing crazy, doing whatever the Thetas told us to, and just basically running around like fools. Thank goodness it was all coming to an end tomorrow. That's when we were supposed to have our initiation ceremony and officially become Thetas.

But we still had to get through today. And as I stood inside the front office, willing up the power to go outside, I had to remind myself that it was almost over. We were supposed to meet the Thetas after school in the courtyard. I knew they were going to make the most of this last day. Especially Tori.

I glanced over and saw Jasmine and C. J. walking toward the courtyard. They were smiling and laughing. "They make such a cute couple," I mumbled to myself. I was so happy for Jasmine.

I knew they—and almost everybody else on campus—

were coming to the courtyard to watch this little show we had put together to salute our big sisters. It was supposed to be our "coming out" show, even though we weren't officially in.

I was just about to text Alexis to find out where she was when I saw her come running down the sidewalk. She'd parked in the back of the school so the Thetas wouldn't see her coming in. We'd agreed to meet in the office.

"Girl, I'm glad you made it. I was just about to leave you. You know how they get when we're late," I told her.

Alexis was out of breath. "I know. My fourth-period teacher made me stay after and go over my essay with her. I just knew I was gonna get a ticket the way I was racing to get over here."

I looked toward the courtyard. "Well, it looks like we're the last two. Let's go."

Alexis and I made our way over to the rest of our pledge sisters who were already lined up in the courtyard. Tameka frowned up at us as we passed her.

"You guys are about to get us all in trouble, being late," she hissed.

I rolled my eyes. Just because she was probably the first one here didn't give her the right to be getting mad at us.

Alexis and I didn't say anything as we took our places in line. Tori walked to the center of the courtyard.

"Hello, everyone. Thanks for joining us as we present the newest Theta Ladies," she announced. We had to be careful to make sure there was no sign of hazing so we didn't get in any trouble, but the school did allow us to have "presentation shows," which is what this was considered.

Tori had made it clear beforehand that even though she would act like we were already members when she announced us in front of all the students, we hadn't made it in yet. That didn't happen until the special initiation dinner tomorrow night.

Tori introduced us one by one to the crowd of students that had gathered. After that, we sang some stupid song, then did a quick step. The whole thing lasted about fifteen minutes.

I was grateful when I saw the crowd of students start to disperse. I'd noticed Angel standing way off in the back by herself. Performing in front of her made me extremely uncomfortable. I wished she would at least talk to me so I could make sure she was okay.

Jasmine and C. J. were standing right in front of the crowd and I just knew she was going to have something smart to say as Alexis and I approached her.

"What?" I asked as soon as I was in front of her.

She smiled. "I didn't say a word. I told you, if you like it, I like it."

"Thanks, Jasmine," I said. "That means a lot."

She nodded. "But y'all were kinda tight out there," she replied, making reference to our step show.

"Yeah," C. J. echoed. "You girls had it goin' on."

Both Alexis and I blushed. I was about to say something else when I saw the smile fade from Jasmine's face. I turned to see what she was looking at. Tori was sashaying toward us.

"Hello, Jasmine," she said, her gaze fixed on my friend. "Bet you wished you'd never quit now, huh?"

"Really I don't," Jasmine coolly replied.

"Whatever," Tori replied, flicking her hand.

"Tori, come on, chill out," Alexis finally spoke up. "Jasmine was just congratulating us."

Tori scowled at her. "Do I need to remind you that you are not a Theta yet?"

Alexis backed down. I was shocked that she'd even said anything. She usually tried not to ruffle any feathers. But I guess she was just getting tired of Tori, too.

"You know, Alexis, don't even sweat it," Jasmine said. "Tori doesn't faze me at all." She casually turned to C. J. "I gotta go. I have study hall. So I'll talk to you later, okay?" She smiled warmly at him before walking off.

Tori finally noticed C. J. and looked him up and down. "What's up, C. J.? Dang, you're looking good."

C. J. stared at her, a confused look across his face. "I didn't even know you knew my name."

Tori put her hand to her chest, feigning shock. "Why, C. J., I'm hurt that you would say something like that."

"Yeah right, Tori."

"So, it's like that?" Tori laughed. "Whatever." She was

about to walk off when she stopped, and looked skeptically at Alexis.

"You know, since you wanna talk back to me, I need you to entertain me." She looked like she had some diabolical plan dancing in her head.

"Entertain you? How?" Alexis asked, her voice shaky. I didn't know what Tori was up to, but it didn't sound good.

Tori glanced back at C. J. "Go give C. J. a kiss."

Both my and Alexis's eyes widened in horror.

"Excuse me?" Alexis said.

"I didn't stutter," Tori snapped. "Kiss C. J. now. And on the lips. A French kiss." She smiled.

"I'm not doing that."

"You will if you want to be a Theta." Tori folded her arms across her chest. "And you have one minute." Several other Thetas had started to gather around. I was hoping somebody would step in and say or do something. But as usual when Tori was on a rampage, nobody said anything.

Alexis looked at me, her eyes tearing up. I knew exactly what she was thinking. C. J. was Jasmine's man and that meant he was off-limits, even for a pledge prank.

"Tori, chill," C. J. finally said.

Some guy standing behind C. J. pushed his shoulder. "Man, don't be a punk. That girl is fine."

"Yeah," another boy echoed. "Man up!"

"Shoot, I'll kiss her!" somebody else yelled.

"Shut up!" Tori snapped to the onlookers. Her eyes tore into C. J. "If you want Alexis to make it into the Theta Ladies, you'll let her plant one on you. Good grief, it's just a stupid kiss." She spun to Alexis. "Do it now!"

C. J. looked like he really didn't want to do it. He really didn't know Alexis, and all the boys standing behind him, egging him on, was getting to him.

Alexis slowly walked up to C. J. She had her head lowered and she looked like she was desperately fighting back tears.

"Jasmine ain't even here. Dang," Tori spat. "Just kiss him and get it over with. And I wanna see some tongue. Not those old grandma kisses."

"Tori . . ." I spoke up, trying to plead with her.

She cut her eyes at me. "You're not a Theta yet either. So I suggest you mind your business." She turned back to Alexis. "If I have to tell you one more time . . ."

Alexis raised her head, her eyes meeting C. J.'s. She took a deep breath, closed her eyes, then leaned in and quickly kissed him on the lips before backing up.

"*French* kiss." Tori giggled. "Don't you know what a French kiss is?"

Alexis sighed, then leaned back in, kissing him again. This time she parted her lips and let her tongue quickly intertwine with C. J.'s.

She stood back after she was finished and turned toward Tori. "There, are you happy?" Her voice was about to crack.

Tori leaned over and looked across the courtyard. Jasmine was standing there, her mouth open, her backpack hanging loosely by her side. I could see the shock on her face as she looked back and forth between C. J. and Alexis.

"Jasmine!" Alexis held her hand up to her mouth. "Oh no!"

Even from across the grassy courtyard, I could see Jasmine's chest heaving up and down. She shook her head in disgust, threw down a cell phone she was holding in her hand, then spun around and raced out of the courtyard. C. J. took off after her, calling her name as he tried to catch her.

A wide smile crossed Tori's face. "Did you ask me was I happy?" she said, glancing in the direction Jasmine had run. "Very. I'm very happy. I just hoped someone would tell her. The fact that she saw it is gravy." She turned back to Alexis. "Congratulations, Alexis. It looks like you do have what it takes to be a Theta."

14

Jasmine

If either of them knew what was good for them, they would get out of my face.

Both Alexis and C. J. had been calling me all night. Then Camille had played stalker at school all day today. Even Tameka had followed me during lunchtime trying to talk to me. But I wasn't trying to hear nothing none of them had to say.

Alexis kissing C. J. was the ultimate low, and nothing any of them said could change that.

I knew they were going to try to use tonight's Good Girlz meeting to beg my forgiveness. But they might as well not even waste their breath.

As I suspected, Alexis, Camille, and Tameka were standing by the door as soon as I walked into the room.

Alexis had tears in her eyes. I shot her a look to let her know I wasn't moved.

"Just let me explain," she whimpered.

"Explain what?" I angrily shrugged. "Let me guess: the Thetas made you do it."

Alexis lowered her eyes to the floor. "They did."

"And of course, being a Theta is more important than our friendship. More important than me getting hurt, right?"

Tameka took a step toward me. "Come on, Jaz. You know Alexis didn't mean anything. It's all just part of the process."

"Uggghhh!" I huffed as I stomped over to the window. "I am so sick and tired of hearing that mess about it being part of the process." I spun around to face them. "What part of 'I don't care what the Thetas told you to do' do you not get? What you did was foul. Low-down! If I hadn't forgotten to give C. J. back his phone, I would've never come back. What then? Would you all just have pretended it never happened? You know someone was bound to tell me!"

Tameka walked over to the window and stood in front of me again. "It was just a stupid kiss. You know it didn't mean anything," she said.

I bit down on my bottom lip, trying to keep from going off. "Tameka, you would want to get out of my face." I finally replied through gritted teeth.

I guess my expression told her I wasn't playing because she backed down.

I looked at Camille, surprised that she hadn't said anything yet.

"Jasmine, you don't know how sorry I am," Alexis repeated for the twelve thousandth time.

"Put on a new song because that one is getting old," I replied.

"But it's the truth." Alexis wiped away the stream of tears trickling down her face. "You know I love you like you're my blood sister. And I would never intentionally hurt you."

I angrily rolled my eyes. I was mad as all get-out, so why in the world did I find myself feeling sorry for her?

"Why?" I asked after staring at her for a few minutes.

"Nobody even knew you and C. J. were together," Tameka interjected.

I cut my eyes at her. "Stop talking to me, Tameka." I turned back to Alexis. "Besides, Alexis knew. Didn't you?"

She nodded.

I was tired of arguing with them so I just threw up my arms. "That was messed up what you did, Alexis. You let Tori play you. She was just trying to hurt me and you helped her do it."

Alexis nodded again like a child being scolded by her parents.

"It wasn't like that," Camille finally said. "I think Tori's demand caught Alexis off guard and she didn't know what to do."

"How about telling Tori to go to he—"

"I just know you're not about to curse in the Lord's

house." Rachel stood in the doorway, her hands perched on her hips.

I couldn't help the guilty look that crept up on my face. But I was actually grateful to see Rachel come in the door because Alexis was really starting to get to me. Now, as far as I was concerned, this conversation was over.

"Good Lord," Rachel sighed as she walked into the room. "Somebody wanna tell me what drama we are dealing with today?"

I glared at Alexis. She was looking all pathetic.

"Please forgive me," she said, sniffing.

I sighed, frustrated that my anger toward her seemed to have all but disappeared.

"You know, just squash it. I know you don't want C. J., Alexis, but that was still jacked up what you did. But I'm done talking about it."

I walked back over to my seat, for once looking forward to Rachel starting her weekly lesson.

Rachel, of course, wouldn't let up, so Tameka filled her in on everything that happened. I guess Rachel knew talking about it would only make it worse because, thankfully, she just let it drop and instead started talking about upcoming community service projects.

I tuned her out as I began thinking of all the stuff the Good Girlz had been through. The time we took a road trip to find Angel and almost got abducted by some psychos, the shoplifting, my search for my dad, the talk show . . . the list goes on. We'd been through a lot together and we'd come through it all tighter than ever.

But I had a sickening feeling that our friendship might not be able to survive the Thetas.

15

Jasmine

"Jasminium Nichelle Solé Jones! Telephone!"

My brother Jaheim was bellowing my name at the top of his lungs. My full name. The name that I hated and he knew that I hated.

"It's the stalker, C. J.!" Jaheim yelled. As if I asked him to be my personal message taker and screen my calls with his nosy behind.

"I said, I'm coming!" I shouted back from the bathroom at the end of the hallway, where I'd been washing my hair.

"Well, you'd betta hurry up because you know you ain't allowed to have phone calls after nine. Mama gon' beat your butt," he cackled. I'm sure that announcement was for the benefit of C. J. I so could not wait to move out. I had it already planned. I was bouncing on my eighteenth birthday, which couldn't come a moment too soon.

I wrapped a towel around my hair and made my way down the hallway to the living room, where Jaquan,

Jalen, and Jaheim sat around in their usual spots, playing PlayStation.

"Where's the cordless phone?" I snapped to no one in particular. No one bothered to answer me.

I walked in front of the TV, blocking the game.

"Move!" Jaheim ordered.

"I said, where's the phone?"

"I don't know. Jaquan had it!" Jaheim yelled. "Move your big butt out the way before you make me lose!"

I wanted to tell him he was already a loser, but I spotted the phone on the end table.

"Ooops!" I said as my foot "accidentally" got tangled in the PlayStation's power cord and pulled it out of the wall. I briefly looked at the blank TV screen. "Sorry, it looks like I messed up your game," I sweetly said. I ignored my brothers screaming as I sashayed over, snatched up the phone, and made my way back to the bedroom.

I really didn't care that I had kept C. J. waiting all this time because I was still mad at him. The only reason I was taking his call now was because he'd been blowing up my phone since I saw him locking lips with Alexis two days ago. He'd run after me then, but I'd ditched study hall and hopped on the bus before he could catch up to me.

I didn't want to talk to him at all but he wasn't giving up. He called so much yesterday that my mom told him to stop. The fact that he called again today anyway and risked her wrath meant he was pretty desperate. So I decided to at least try to hear him out.

"Are you flunking English or something?" I said into the mouthpiece.

C. J. paused, like he was surprised I actually came to the phone. "What?" he finally said.

"I said, are you flunking English?"

"Huh? English? What does that have to do with anything?"

I plopped down on my bed, pulling my fluffy Hello Kitty pillow up under my chin. "You must be flunking English, because obviously you don't understand it very well. So let me break it down for you one last time. Lose. My. Number."

"Come on, Jasmine. Don't be like that." He was trying to sound all sincere. But I was hip to his game. "I told you a hundred times I'm sorry," he said.

"And I told you a hundred times, I don't care." I tightened the towel around my head so I didn't get my pillow wet.

"Why are you being like this?"

"Being like what, C. J.? You kissed my best friend. Am I supposed to be okay with that?"

"But it wasn't even like that," he pleaded. "You know that."

"I don't know nothing except what I saw." I knew I'd

let Alexis off the hook—somewhat, anyway—but that's because she was my girl. C. J., he was just a stank, dirty dog who had proven he was just like the rest of the stank, dirty dogs.

"What was I supposed to do, Jasmine?"

I got loud. "How 'bout push her off of you! Tell Tori to kiss your . . ." I blew a frustrated breath as I tried to calm myself down. "You come at me, talking all this mess about how you're a man now," I said, my voice a lot softer. "If you were a man, you wouldn't have let Tori or your boys punk you into kissing Alexis. If you were a man, you would've said, 'You know, this just might hurt Jasmine, the girl I claim I want to be with.' "

"I know. And I'm sorry."

"You are sorry, C. J. But not half as sorry as I am that I even thought about giving you a chance. Now, for the last time. Lose. My. Number." I slammed the Off button on the phone. I held it in my hands for a few minutes, half expecting it to ring again. I couldn't help but feel my heart drop when after fifteen minutes, it didn't.

16

Jasmine

It was hot as all get-out and I so did not want to be at the stupid state fair. It had been just over twenty-four hours since I hung up on C. J. and he hadn't called back. I was really bummed out. So a fair was the last place I felt like being.

This was the first time the Texas State Fair was being held in Houston and guess who got stuck taking her lame brothers to the big event? My mother hadn't given me much choice. She'd told me to take my three younger brothers to the fair or stay home and clean the house from top to bottom. I'd almost taken the housecleaning versus a whole evening with my brothers, but that pile of nasty dishes made me change my mind. It would be just my luck that I'd take them to the fair, and still have to wash those dishes when I got home.

"Come on, Jasmine," six-year-old Jalen yelled. "I wanna ride the Ferris wheel."

"Boy, I told you, you can't ride but three rides. These tickets ain't free."

"Mama gave us twenty dollars each," eleven-year-old Jaheim snapped.

"Yeah, and one ride costs nearly five bucks," I snapped back.

My mother had shocked us when she came home with free tickets to the fair and money for us to go. As broke as we stayed, I sure couldn't see how she was shelling out nearly a hundred dollars for us to go to the fair. But she'd explained that her boss had not only given her the tickets, but he'd also given her the money for us to spend.

"Why you gotta hold the money anyway?" Jaheim said as he stuck his bottom lip out like a two-year-old.

" 'Cause you'd lose it or spend it before we got in the fair good."

"Well, I saw that fifty-dollar bill you took out from under your bed," Jaheim announced.

Jaheim was a true pain in the butt. His spying behind made me sick.

"And? That's my money!" I yelled. I'd made some money passing out fliers for Alexis's dad. And I saved almost every nickel and dime I got. I hated bringing that whole fifty-dollar bill but I didn't have any change. I tried to keep big bills in my secret stash; that way I couldn't easily spend it. But I dang sure didn't want my brothers knowing I had money hidden anywhere. And now it looked like I had to find a new hiding place, thanks to Jaheim.

"You can pay for us to ride a couple of more rides," Jalen whined.

"I wish I would," I responded.

"Man, you jacked up." Jaheim held his hand out. "Give us the money to go buy some tickets for the roller coaster."

I handed them a twenty. I debated giving them all of the money Mama had given us. Shoot, the sooner they spent all the money, the sooner we could go home.

My oldest brother, Jaquan, had already taken off to go mack on girls. I found myself wishing I had called Alexis or Camille to come with me so I wouldn't be so freakin' bored.

I stood idly around for a few minutes before deciding to go get a funnel cake. I had been in line about five minutes when Tori and her crew walked up. I fought back a groan. I was not in the mood for her. And if she knew what was best for her, she would just leave me alone.

"Well, looky here, girls," Tori said as she stopped right in front of me. "If it isn't the Theta Ladies reject."

I took a deep breath. Why wouldn't people let me walk away from my violent ways?

"Last time I checked, I rejected Theta Ladies. They didn't reject me," I said, trying not to catch an attitude. "And why are you in my face?"

Tori ignored me and kept talking. "Oh, excuse me. You just dropped out because you couldn't take the heat. Your other little chica friend was the one we rejected." She and her friends laughed.

I raised my eyebrows. "My *chica* friend?"

"Yeah, the little Mexican," Tori said as she flung her long, wavy brown hair over her shoulder.

"Are you talking about Angel?" I asked.

"*Sí.*" Tori cackled.

"Oh, you think that's funny? You got something against Hispanics?"

Tori looked around at her friends and rolled her eyes. "Not at all, except the fact that they're trying to take over everything as it is and I'm not about to let them take over Theta Ladies."

I stared at her. That had to be the dumbest thing I'd heard in a long time. "What is that supposed to mean?"

Tori shrugged. "It means what it means. We don't want any Mexicans in our organization. Just like we didn't want any big Amazon-looking warriors."

I ignored her dig at me because I was dumbfounded by her racist statement.

"Excuse me, is this 2008 or 1968? I'm confused. You have the nerve to be prejudiced?"

"Call me what you want. I just know that your little friend needs to go join the Omega Chica Cantina or something."

Her friends started laughing like that corny stuff was really funny.

"Angel is one of the nicest people you'll ever meet. I don't believe you actually rejected her because of her race!"

Tori folded her arms across her chest. "Believe it. We're selective about who we let in. No *chicas* and no Amazons."

Okay, I gave her a pass on the first Amazon comment, but she was asking for it now. I was just about to reach out and knock the mess out of her when the woman at the funnel cake counter bellowed, "May I help you?"

I looked at the people behind me, a young Hispanic couple who obviously had been listening to the conversation. They looked just as disgusted with Tori as I did. I motioned for them to go ahead in front of me and order as I stepped aside.

"You know, Tori, I was two seconds from sending you to the dentist, but I realized you're not worth it. You're a sorry snob who has to put other people down in order to lift yourself up. In your wildest dreams you couldn't be half the woman that Angel is."

"Ooooh, I'm so scared of your threats." She laughed.

I could only shake my head in pity as I walked off without ordering my funnel cake. Tori had definitely made me lose my appetite.

I had to get to Camille and Alexis. If this news didn't make them see my point about the Thetas, I didn't know what would.

17

Camille

$\mathcal{I}$ sat with my mouth open. I couldn't believe what Jasmine had said. She'd just finished filling everyone in on her little run-in with Tori this past weekend. We were at our regular Good Girlz meeting waiting to begin finalizing details for our big community service project, a trip to New Orleans to help Habitat for Humanity rebuild homes devastated by Hurricane Katrina. We were among several youth organizations across the city who were taking part in a Houston program called "Teens Giving Back." So we had to iron out details. But right now, I was more interested in what Jasmine was saying.

"So you mean to tell me they rejected Angel because she's Hispanic?" I asked in disbelief.

"I didn't stutter," Jasmine snapped. She folded her arms and shook her head. "I told you they were no good."

Angel sat off to the side, stunned. We were all happy to see her at tonight's meeting. She'd come in with a good attitude, and told us from the jump that she was putting the Thetas' rejection behind her. But this news must've definitely hurt. "Wow. I was nothing but nice to them the whole time and I never stood a chance because I'm Hispanic? That's messed up," she softly said.

"Tell me about it," Jasmine said, rolling her eyes.

"Are you sure?" Alexis asked Jasmine.

"Are you deaf?" she snapped. "I told you exactly what Tori said."

I hesitated before saying, "Well, Tori is just one person." I could tell Jasmine was mad. But she needed to see the Thetas were bigger than Tori.

"Camille, quit making excuses for them!"

"Jasmine, she's right," Alexis chimed in. "I know Tori is foul, but I just don't believe all of them are like that."

Jasmine stared at Alexis in disbelief. "Being biracial, this should make you madder than anyone else," she said.

Alexis looked away like she didn't know what to say.

Tameka sucked her teeth. "Just because Tori is a jerk doesn't mean they all are." She didn't seem as shocked at the news. Or maybe she just didn't care, but I wouldn't be surprised if she already knew and had just kept quiet.

Jasmine cut her eyes at us. "Boy, they got you all brainwashed already. They're like a gang or something."

I was just about to say something when Alexis stopped me. She motioned toward the empty seat where Angel had previously sat. "Guys . . ."

In the midst of our arguing, we hadn't even noticed that Angel had slipped out of the room.

"She probably couldn't stand listening to you guys take up for those clowns," Jasmine said. "And I'm beginning to know just how she feels. It's bad enough they have you stabbing your friends in the back." She narrowed her eyes at Alexis. "Now you find out they're racists and you're okay with that?"

"It's not okay," I said, massaging my forehead. I was still trying to digest everything Jasmine said. If it was true, did I really want to be associated with a group like that?

"Should we go and try and find Angel?" Alexis asked after a few seconds of silence.

Before we could answer, Rachel appeared in the doorway. She had a concerned look across her face. "Does somebody want to tell me why Angel just tore out of here in tears?"

Jasmine pursed her lips and turned toward me. "Well?"

I blew out a deep breath and said, "Angel just found out that she didn't make it into the Theta Ladies because she's Hispanic."

"What?" Rachel said.

"Yeah, those grimy snobs said my girl was the wrong race to be a Theta."

Jasmine's nasty comments were getting to me, and I was getting worried about Angel.

"That's why I told them they didn't need to be Thetas," Jasmine continued.

"Jasmine, that's enough," Rachel said. "I get the picture." She sighed heavily. "All this sorority stuff is proving to be more trouble than it's worth."

"Tell me about it," Jasmine muttered.

"Jasmine, I told you, that's enough," Rachel replied. "How do you all know that's why Angel didn't make it?"

I looked at Jasmine and waited for her to answer. "Tell her about Tori," I finally said.

Jasmine shook her head and stuck out her lips. "Uh-uh. She told me to be quiet."

Rachel shook her head. "Quit being silly and tell me what happened."

Jasmine huffed, then recapped her story. While she was filling Rachel in, my mind replayed all the times we'd been around the Thetas. They had barely acknowledged Angel, and when they did, they'd treated her like crap. I guess they never had any intention of letting her in.

"Well, I can see why Angel is upset," Rachel said after Jasmine finished her story. "It's hard to believe that in 2008, there is still prejudice like this, especially among young people."

"Jasmine, you know you don't like the Thetas anyway. Maybe they were just messing with you and you took them seriously," Tameka interjected.

"And maybe I'm America's Next Top Model," Jasmine shot back.

Rachel looked sadly at us. "Girls, this just breaks my

heart. You all have formed a wonderful bond over the years. You can't control other people's prejudices, but you can control your own. I sure hope you don't condone this behavior."

"They might as well," Jasmine snapped. "And that's really jacked up."

I finally spoke up. "Miss Rachel, it's not fair. Jasmine wants us to drop out of the Thetas, but why should we be penalized because of someone else's prejudices? It's like you said, we can't control what other people think or the way they act."

"But why would you even want to be associated with them? And does that mean you're going to stop being friends with Angel? Because it's obvious the Thetas don't want anyone in their little circle that's not like them," Jasmine said before I could answer the first question.

I sighed, not bothering to answer. It wasn't like anything I said would change her mind anyway. I just knew one thing for sure: Angel was my girl. And if the Thetas *had* rejected her because she's Hispanic, I didn't know what I was going to do.

18

Camille

$\mathcal{I}$ couldn't get Jasmine's words out of my mind. But then I kept hoping Tameka was right and Jasmine had blown this all out of proportion. I knew Tori could be a witch, but I just didn't want to believe she'd go that far.

"Tori, I need to talk to you," I said as I caught up with her in the cafeteria at the beginning of lunch.

She stopped before getting in the food line and turned to me. As usual, she was surrounded by several other Thetas.

"Is it true that you all rejected Angel because she's Mexican?" I asked. Usually, I would've been a little scared of Tori, of the power she had to make me a Theta or crush my dream, but today I was too worked up to be scared. I'd spent all night calling Angel, and she wouldn't take my calls. I couldn't half sleep, this was bothering me so much.

Tori huffed and rolled her eyes. She didn't immediately answer me. Instead, she took her time, pulled down her jean miniskirt, then adjusted her fuchsia and black layered

T-shirts. Finally, she looked at me and said, "I guess your girl couldn't wait to come running back to tell you that."

"Is it true or not?" I firmly asked

Tori turned up her nose. "You'd better watch your tone. I know you've been accepted and everything, but it's not too late for me to revoke your membership."

I hesitated. I couldn't believe that as bad as I wanted to be a Theta, I now found myself questioning that decision.

Alisha, another member who seemed to be Tori's side-kick, stepped toward me. "Camille, we are very proud to have you and all the other girls we selected. I know you're friends with Jasmine and Angel. But you need to realize that we're your sisters now. And your loyalty lies with your sisters."

I was starting to feel bad. I didn't want them to think I was being disloyal. But I wanted to be loyal to Angel, too. I decided to try another approach.

"I guess I just don't understand why you would keep someone out just because of that," I said, softening my tone.

"I don't understand why Angel even wants to be a part of a black sorority," Tori retorted.

"Because she doesn't see color," I replied.

"Look," Tori said, like she couldn't believe she was even wasting her time debating this. "There are plenty of Hispanic groups for Angel to join. Why does she have to be a member of our organization?"

"Why do we have to discriminate?" I countered.

Tori blew a disgusted breath. "You know, I don't even want to debate this. As long as I'm president, Angel and anyone like her will not be a Theta." She flicked me off and walked away.

"Yeah," Alisha added, as she stepped in my face. "You need to decide if you really want to be a Theta. And if you do, I suggest you recognize that some things just can't be changed." She shot me a hateful look before turning and taking off after Tori.

I was sick. I could tell there was no getting through to Tori. I could still hear Jasmine's words: *Why would you even want to be a part of a racist organization like that?*

I had to remind myself, this was bigger than Tori. She was graduating this year. I'd get in, work hard, then change that stupid mind-set. *Yeah, that's the solution*, I thought as I went to grab something to eat.

A smile crept up on my face for the first time in days. I had a good feeling that this was all going to work out after all.

19

Camille

I was so relieved to see Angel at school today. Me, Alexis, and Jasmine had been calling her for two days, but she had her mom tell us she wasn't really up to talking. She said she'd just see us at school, only we never did.

I was standing in the hall talking to some other Theta members when I spotted Angel. I told them bye and took off to catch up with Angel.

"Hey, Angel," I said, just as she was about to turn the corner.

"Hey." She stopped and looked me up and down. Her tone was definitely different. It was cold, like she had an attitude.

"Are you mad at me?" I asked.

She shrugged nonchalantly. "Why would I be mad at you?"

"Because of this whole Theta mess."

She shook her head. "Don't sweat it. As Jasmine would say, it is what it is."

"I'm really sorry."

"No need for you to apologize. You had nothing to do with it."

"I know, but I still feel bad."

"Don't feel bad." Angel glanced up at four Hispanic girls who were standing a few feet away, staring at us like they were waiting on someone. I knew one of them—this messy girl named Christina who was always starting trouble. I recognized the others from around school, but I didn't remember their names.

"Well, I gotta go. Christina and 'em are waiting on me."

I know a strange look crossed my face. Since when did Angel start hanging out with Christina and her friends?

Angel didn't give me time to ask any questions as she darted off.

Angel's attitude and her new friendships bugged me the rest of the day. I'd tried to ask Jasmine about it during our history class, but she acted like she was still mad at me and I wasn't about to kiss her butt.

I decided I would just wait on Angel after school so we could talk then. When the last bell rang, I hurried straight to Angel's Algebra II class. By the time I got there, she was already gone, so I headed down the hall to her locker. I spotted her laughing with Christina and a couple of other girls.

"Hey Angel," I said, approaching her. "What's up?"

I was about to speak to the other girls, but the looks on their faces stopped me cold.

"Why don't you go find out what's up with the Thetas?" Christina finally snapped. She was a pretty girl, but had this rough look, like she'd been around the block a few times. She wore her silky black hair pulled back in a ponytail. And she was dressed like a tomboy in some baggy Dickies, a black T-shirt, and some hi-top Converse.

I decided to ignore Christina and turned my attention back to Angel. "Can I talk to you, in private?"

Angel shot me a nonchalant expression. "Nah, anything you say to me you can say in front of my friends."

Friends? To my knowledge, she didn't even half know these girls. Since when did they become her friends?

"Angel, what's going on?" I lowered my voice and asked her. "We're tight. Talk to me. What's all this about?"

Christina stepped up right next to Angel. "It looks like Angel wants to stick with 'her own kind'—you know, like your little sorority members feel she should do."

I stood speechless.

"Oh yeah, we know all about the Thetas having a problem with Mexicans," Christina continued when I didn't say anything. "I guess y'all think because you're black, you're better than us or something?"

I hated that Angel had told these girls about her being rejected and why. I knew that meant nothing but trouble.

"Nobody thinks that." I know I didn't sound convincing.

"Save it," Christina spat. "We already know the deal. We confronted your funky sorority members already, and they admitted to it, told Angel to stick with her kind, and so that's what she's doing. So bounce."

I looked at Angel, hoping she'd speak up. But the look on her face told me Christina was speaking for her.

"Angel . . ."

Christina moved closer to me. "Bounce," she repeated.

Since I wasn't trying to fight nobody, and it was obvious Angel wasn't in her right mind right now, I left.

I couldn't believe Tori had just straight out admitted the real reason they rejected Angel. What was she thinking? Our school was about half black and half Hispanic, so the last thing we needed was some racial problems. But judging from the mean mugs on Christina and her friends' faces, it looked like there were definitely about to be some problems.

20

Camille

"Hel-lo." Kalvin waved his hand in my face. "Are you even listening to me?"

I snapped out of my daze. Kalvin and I were walking down the hallway between classes. I had tried to talk to him about how upset I was over Angel, but as usual, he switched the focus back on him and was telling me about something that happened at football practice. He was so not the prize I'd initially thought he was. I'd zoned out of his conversation as my mind drifted back to Angel.

"You know, I'm not used to girls tuning me out," Kalvin said, stroking his chin.

"I'm sorry. I just have a lot on my mind."

"Obviously." He turned to see what had captured my attention now. It was Angel, walking down the hall laughing and talking with Christina and two other girls.

"Look, handle your business. Holla at me when y'all work all that Theta drama out." Kalvin stomped off. I debated following after him. But I couldn't really deal with Kalvin right now. This whole thing with Angel was getting ridiculous and it was consuming my thoughts.

Angel hadn't hung out with us all week long. She'd been too busy all up under her new so-called best friends. She hadn't returned my phone calls and she hadn't been to a Good Girlz meeting. She'd even been ignoring Miss Rachel's calls. That's why when I watched her walk toward me, I made up my mind: she and I were going to talk and we were going to talk right now.

"Angel, can I holla at you for a minute," I said, stopping her as she approached me.

Before she could respond, Christina stepped in front of her again.

"What do you need to holla at her about?" she said.

I put on a confused look. "I'm sorry. I thought I said, *Angel*, can I holla at you."

Christina wiggled her neck as she stepped in my face. "Well, Angel don't wanna holla at you. *Comprende?*"

I suddenly wished Jasmine was around. Christina was at least five feet, eight inches—a good five inches taller than me. But even though I may have been a little scared, I wasn't going to let her punk me, especially not in front of the nosey crowd of people that had started to gather around us.

"No, I don't '*comprende*,'" I replied. "This is between me and Angel."

"Well, Angel's business is now my business," Christina said defiantly.

I was just about to say something else when Tori, Raquelle, and Alisha walked up. "What's going on, Camille?" Tori asked, eyeing Christina and Angel. "Is there a problem?"

"It's only a problem if you're about to make one," Christina replied as she stared back at Tori.

The last thing I wanted was to get into it with Christina and her friends. And I dang sure didn't want the Thetas getting into any trouble over this. I just wanted to talk to Angel.

"Naw, Tori, I'm straight. I was just trying to talk to Angel, that's all."

Christina laughed as she turned toward one of her friends and said, *"Ella necesita hablar a esa muchacha negra acerca de que alzó teje."*

I had no idea what she said, but the way they were looking at Tori and laughing, it had to have been about her. Tori must've sensed it, too, because she stepped closer to Christina.

"What did you just say?"

Christina just kept laughing.

"She said something about a negra," said Alisha.

"Are you calling me names?" Tori said, balling up her fists. I didn't take her for the fighting type, but I knew she wouldn't let Christina punk her.

Raquelle commented, "She said that Camille needed to

be talking to, and I quote, that black wench about her jacked-up weave." She cocked her head and stared at Christina. "You're not the only one who can speak Spanish."

The smile left Christina's face. "*And?* I don't care if she knows what I said."

I knew I needed to do something or things were about to get straight-up ugly in here. "Y'all, chill. This is between me and Angel." I looked at Angel, who had been silent this whole time. "Can we please go somewhere and talk?"

Angel looked at Christina, then at Tori, before turning her attention back to me. "You know, Camille, Christina is right. There's really nothing for us to talk about. You guys have made it clear where I stand, so I don't think we have anything to say to each other."

I stared at her in disbelief. I couldn't believe that we'd come to this. "Angel, this is crazy. We're best friends."

Christina glared at me. "You *were* best friends. But I guess becoming a Theta made your true colors show. Angel can now see you for the racist that you are."

"I'm not racist," I protested. "Angel, you know that."

Christina rolled her eyes as she pointed toward Tori and the other Thetas. "Birds of a feather." She turned and walked away with Angel right behind her.

"Oh, and Miss Thang," Christina said, stopping and turning back toward Tori, "this ain't over. Believe that."

She laughed as she walked off and I couldn't help but get a sick feeling in the pit of my stomach.

21

Camille

Jasmine stared at me like I was stuck on stupid or something. "Come on, Camille, can you really blame Angel for hanging out with Christina and her friends? I mean, what your little stuck-up sorority sisters did was low down. Even you have to admit that."

I sighed. I was still trippin' over Angel's funky attitude. I tried to tell myself she was just mad right now as I stuffed another mozzarella stick into my mouth. We were hanging out at T.G.I. Fridays, along with a ton of other young people.

Me, Jasmine, and Alexis were sitting in a booth sipping on virgin strawberry daiquiris and eating appetizers. It felt good for us all to be hanging out again. The only thing that would've made this just like old times was if Angel had been there.

But that wasn't happening. And it looked more and more like it wouldn't happen ever again.

"I wish you would quit saying that. The Thetas are not stuck up." That's all I could seem to come up with. I didn't have a defense to their reasons behind rejecting Angel. I cut my eyes at Jasmine. "And you forget, we're Thetas now," I said, pointing to Alexis. "So if you talk about them, then you talk about us."

"Then I'm talking about you," Jasmine pointedly said. She was really about to make me mad. Her not liking Tori was one thing but this bashing the Thetas was getting real old. I was just about to tell her that when Alexis pulled my arm.

"Look, there are some AKAs and Deltas," she said, pointing to a large group of women being seated at a long table across from us. They all wore pink-and-green or red-and-white T-shirts.

"Oooh, wow," Jasmine sarcastically said. "I guess that's your next goal in life, to become college sorority girls. Way to strive for what really matters."

"I wonder what they're doing hanging out together. I thought AKAs and Deltas didn't like each other," Alexis continued, totally ignoring Jasmine's sarcastic remarks.

"Alexis, you are so naïve. You watch way too many movies," I told her. "Don't believe everything you hear."

At that moment one of the AKAs spotted us looking at their table and waved like she knew us.

"Oh my goodness, that's Crystal waving at us," Alexis excitedly said.

"Who?" I asked.

"She used to go to my school. She was my senior mentor when I was a freshman," she explained. "Let's go talk to her."

Jasmine frowned up. "Don't even look at me." She stuffed another cheesestick in her mouth. "I don't feel like jockin' nobody today."

Alexis pulled me up from my chair before I had a chance to protest. I was a little skeptical myself about going up to a bunch of strange women asking them dumb questions in the middle of a crowded restaurant, but Alexis seemed determined to talk to them.

"Hey Crystal. Do you remember me? We went to high school together," Alexis babbled.

"Alexis, right?" Crystal replied.

"Yes, and this is my friend Camille. What are you doing here? I thought you were off at college somewhere."

"I am," Crystal replied. "I'm a sophomore at Prairie View A&M. We're just here for the weekend, hanging out."

"Excuse me," one of the women at the table, a Delta, interrupted, "but what is a Theta Lady?" She pointed to our jackets.

"Oh, it's the sorority at our high school," I said proudly.

"Oh, that's so cute," another one of them, an AKA, replied. "We didn't have sororities when I was in high school. I had to wait until I got to college."

"So how do you like being in a sorority?" the Delta asked us.

"Well, to be honest," I said, glancing back at our table where Jasmine was sitting, looking more than a little agitated that we left her alone, "it's been great so far, but not everyone is as happy about it as we are."

The girls at the table started to giggle and gave us a "we know how you feel" look. "Girl, get used to that. There are a lot of haters in this world who don't want to see you succeed," Crystal told us. "I take it your friend over there isn't a member?"

"Naw," I said. "Jasmine started out with us, but she quit because they were making her do some really stupid stuff and picking on her." I really did feel bad for Jasmine. I know she tries to act all hard, but deep down, she really wanted to be liked and accepted.

"Good for her," another Delta replied. "I can't believe hazing has made it all the way down to the high schools. It's just stupid. Y'all do know that's not what being a part of a sorority is all about, don't you?"

Alexis and I both looked at each other. "Well, yeah, we know there are other things, community service and stuff," I said. "But what else were we supposed to do? We didn't want to get kicked out before we even made it," I added defensively. I was beginning to feel a little dejected after talking to them. And a little angry with Alexis for dragging me over here.

"I thought being in a sorority would be fun," Alexis added. "But it's causing all kinds of problems, especially because another one of our friends didn't make it either, and we think it's because she's Hispanic. Now she's barely even speaking to us."

I didn't understand why Alexis was telling them all of our business but before I could shoot her a look telling her to chill, Jasmine cleared her throat loudly from our table. I guess that was her way of signaling to us that it was time for us to cut the conversation short.

"Well, ladies, they just brought our food so I guess we should get back to our table," I said.

I was about to turn and walk off when Alexis quickly spoke. "Crystal, I know this may be a lot to ask, but we also belong to a youth group called the Good Girlz at Zion Hill Missionary Baptist Church. I was wondering if you and some of your friends wouldn't mind coming to one of our meetings to talk to us and maybe answer some questions about sorority life. Maybe that will help ease some of the problems between us. I mean, we'd have to make sure it was okay with Miss Rachel, our sponsor, but I'm sure she won't mind at all."

Crystal smiled at us and replied, "I think that's a good idea. I know some of my sorors and other Greek members would love to come talk to your group." All the other women at the table nodded in agreement. "The majority of what all sororities do, not just AKAs and Deltas, is community service. Mentoring young girls is one of our projects, so that works perfect for us."

Alexis excitedly pulled out her iPhone. "Great!" she said. "If you give me your number, I'll have Miss Rachel call you to set it all up."

Crystal programmed her number into Alexis's phone and we went back to our table. I just knew Jasmine was going to have something smart to say. I was right. Before we could even sit down good, she started in.

"Y'all know you wrong for leaving me sitting at the table, looking like I'm out to eat by myself. But I'ma let y'all slide. This time. And only because Alexis is paying for dinner." She dug into her chicken fingers.

"I am?" Alexis said.

"This was your idea," Jasmine said. "You know I don't have no money."

"I guess I am then." Alexis smiled.

Jasmine took another sip of her drink, then said, "I guess you feel better now since you talked to those uppity sorority girls."

"For your information, they were not uppity," I said. "They were very down-to-earth and very helpful. As a matter of fact, Alexis invited them to come to one of our Good Girlz meetings to speak and they agreed."

"Good grief," Jasmine complained. "It's bad enough I have to deal with this mess at school, but now I have to deal with it at the Good Girlz meetings? When will this nonsense ever end? Let me know when they're coming so I can make sure I stay home that night."

I shook my head in frustration. I knew Jasmine was serious, just like I knew getting Angel there was going to be a task in itself. Honestly, I didn't know what good the sorority members would do by coming to a meeting, but I figured we had to do something to make everything right again. And this was going to be the first step.

22

Jasmine

Will things ever be the same again? That's the thought that swirled through my mind as I lay in bed. Thankfully, everyone in my family was gone and I had the house to myself for a change so I was able to enjoy some peace and quiet. But now the silence had my mind running rampant. I couldn't help but think about what was happening with my circle of friends.

Even though we'd hung out last night, tonight Camille and Alexis were off somewhere doing Theta stuff and Angel had a new group of friends. Our community service project was coming up and that should definitely give us a chance to bond, but I missed the four of us just hanging out and doing stuff together. Shoot, I even missed Tameka, who was now Tori's flunky. And now with this big black/Hispanic division, the chances of us all hanging out together were looking slimmer and slimmer.

"Maybe Miss Rachel can give me some advice," I mumbled, picking up the phone to call her. I punched in her cell phone number and was grateful when she answered on the second ring.

"Hi, Miss Rachel, it's Jasmine. I hope it's not too late to be calling. I really need to talk to you about something," I said.

"You know it's never too late for my girls," Rachel replied. "Just hold on a moment." I heard some shuffling, then she yelled, "Jordan, I'm going to tell you one last time, turn off that video game and go to bed before I beat your behind!"

I chuckled at Miss Rachel, who reminded me of my own mother with her no-nonsense approach to discipline. The only difference was, I could talk to Miss Rachel about anything—something I definitely couldn't do with my mother.

"So, what's the problem, Jasmine?" Rachel asked when she returned to the phone.

I sighed heavily, trying to figure out where to begin. "I'm having some serious issues with the other members of the group and I'm not sure what to do about it. Camille, Alexis, and Tameka are all wrapped up in the Theta Ladies and Angel has started hanging with a new group of girls at school," I explained. "Ever since Angel found out the real reason she didn't make it into that stupid sorority, nothing has been the same."

Rachel was silent, like she was thinking about her

answer carefully before responding. "I think it's really sad that hate that my parents grew up with is still out there. It's proof that although we've come a long way, we still have a way to go. But there is no generation better equipped to change that climate of hate than you guys."

"Well, joinin' the Theta ladies ain't the way to do it."

"I'm not saying Camille and Alexis should choose Angel over the Thetas, but they cannot in any shape, form, or fashion tolerate such hate," Rachel said.

"I know, and Tori was saying some pretty hateful things, like Mexicans are taking over everything. It's just jacked up."

"It really is," Rachel replied. "And Camille, Alexis, and even Tameka need to make it clear where they stand on that issue. I will make sure I tell them that. But maybe you can be the one to get people to—instead of focusing on all the negative aspects of things like illegal immigration—look at all that they contribute to the economy and society once they get here, and how to better integrate them, rather than insisting or hoping that they go home."

I knew Miss Rachel was right, but it didn't seem like it would be that easy. A lot of damage had already been done.

"I see your point, Miss Rachel," I said, "but this whole situation might have really messed up our friendship."

"Jasmine," Rachel continued, "I want you to understand

that friends go through their ups and downs all the time. It's not going to always be wonderful between you guys. You've seen that already behind that whole fiasco when you were going out for that teen talk show."

I nodded as I recalled that nightmare. That had definitely taken its toll on our friendship. Shoot, it had almost ended it. Camille had taken backstabbing to a whole new level when we all tried out to host this teen talk show on Channel 2. Luckily, we made up after Camille got fired and came back apologizing to us.

"And you know with that," Rachel continued, snapping me out of my thoughts, "it seemed like you guys would never be friends again. But you got through it. Just like you'll get through this. Honestly, you seem to be the only levelheaded one right now, so you're going to need to keep up the fight to bring everyone back together."

"What am I supposed to do?"

"I don't know. Keep trying to get through to them. Come up with a plan. Anything. Just don't give up on your friendship."

I exhaled and squeezed my eyes shut. I couldn't believe *I* was the one who needed to be levelheaded. As hot tempered as I was?

"Okay, Miss Rachel, I'll think about what you're saying, but I don't know what I can do," I told her.

"I'm confident you'll come up with something. You guys are too good of friends."

"I'm glad somebody's confident," I mumbled.

"What did you say?"

"Nothing," I replied, massaging my temple. "I hear what you're saying. I'll do what I can and I'll let you know what happens."

"All right. You call me back if you need anything."

I said good-bye and hung up the phone.

After a few minutes of lying across my bed, I decided to take Miss Rachel's advice and make the first move to get us back together. I didn't worry about Tameka because in my opinion, she was too far gone. But I did call Camille and Alexis to see if they were back home yet. They were and after talking to them on three-way for a few minutes, we all decided it would be a good idea to go catch a movie tomorrow or something. The hard part was going to be getting Angel to let her guard down long enough to spend time with us. Of course, neither one of them wanted to be the one to call Angel so I had to do it.

I hung up with them, then took another deep breath as I dialed Angel's number. It probably was best that I be the one to call her since I was the only one she really didn't have a reason to be mad at.

"Hey, Angel! What's up, girl? I haven't heard from you in a while," I said as soon as she picked up the phone.

"Oh, this isn't Angel, this is her friend Christina. Angel's a little busy right now. Can I take a message?"

I was a little thrown off since I wasn't used to Angel

having any friends other than us and I definitely couldn't appreciate somebody trying to screen her calls.

"No, I'll hold on," I said, trying not to get an attitude. "Can you tell her Jasmine is on the phone?"

"What part of 'she's busy' do you not get?" Christina said.

I had to catch myself because I was about to go straight off. Obviously, she didn't know who she was talking to. And she definitely must be crazy if she thought she was going to come in and take my—our—place in Angel's life.

"What, are you her personal secretary now?" I said, "I said, I'll hold on."

"Whatever!" Christina mumbled. Then she yelled, "Angel, it's some girl on the phone for you named Jasmine."

A few minutes later Angel got on the phone.

"Oh hey, Jasmine. What's up?" Angel's tone was dry. I absolutely was about to get an attitude now. I hadn't done anything to her so she didn't need to be getting funky with me.

"Why is Christina answering your phone?" I asked.

"She's just helping me with Angelica. What's the big deal?"

I was a little bothered by Angel having some strange new chick around Angelica, but I didn't want to get into that conversation with her so I decided to just leave it alone. If she wanted some stranger around her baby then that was her business.

I told her about me, Camille, and Alexis wanting to go check out a movie tomorrow, just like old times.

"I'll have to check my schedule and get back with you. I think we're goin' to a party over near Sharpstown," Angel said.

I stood up and began pacing my bedroom. For some reason, all of us were pretty protective of Angel, probably because she was so nice, naïve, and gullible. So it was starting to bother me that she had just let Christina—who everybody knew was nothing but trouble—into her life.

"Who is '*we*,' and since when do you have a schedule that needs to be checked?" I asked her. She was for real trippin'. "And who has a party on a freakin' Sunday?" I know she wasn't out-and-out lying to me, was she?

"Look, Jasmine, I know you may not realize this, but my life is not defined by my friendship with you, Camille, and Alexis. I do have a life outside of y'all," she huffed.

"*Your life is not defined by us?*" I shouted. "What in the world does that mean?"

She blew out a deep breath like I was getting on her nerves. "Don't be mad because now I have other people in my life who are important to me. If you don't like it, that's your problem."

I was so close to going off on Angel that I literally had to bite my tongue to keep from losing it. I couldn't believe she was acting like this. When we first met her, she would barely look anyone in the eyes, let alone catch herself getting smart with somebody. This new group of friends had really gone to her head and it was taking everything in my power for me not to put her back in her place.

"You know what, Angel? I'm going to hang up this phone now before you make me say something I am gonna regret. You my girl and all, but you need to think about who your real friends are and who has, and always will be, there for you," I told her. "I'm going to chalk this conversation up to you being upset about the whole Theta thing and give you a pass. You give me a call when you come to your senses." I slammed the phone down before she could reply.

So much for me being levelheaded.

23

Camille

I grabbed my duffel bag and threw it over my shoulder. I couldn't believe how excited I was about doing community service. But this wasn't some boring visit to the senior citizens' center. We were actually heading to New Orleans with the Habitat for Humanity "Teens Give Back" project. Although we were traveling as part of the Good Girlz, other people from my school were going, too—including Christina and her crew and Tori and some of the Thetas. I'd been hoping the trip would give me, Alexis, and Jasmine time to repair our bond with Angel, but somehow I doubted we'd have much success with Christina in the way.

I noticed Angel's sister pulling up to drop off Angel. I quickly made my way over to her car.

"Hey, Rosario." I waved after she came to a stop.

"Hey, Camille," she replied. "I haven't seen you in a while."

I looked at Angel to gauge her reaction, but she acted like she hadn't even heard her sister.

"Hey, Sweet Pea," I said, turning to Angelica, who was sitting in her car seat in the back. I leaned in and tickled Angelica's chin. The little girl giggled and almost made me cry when she said, "Hi, 'Mille!"

"I miss you, Pumpkin," I replied, tousling her curly black hair. "But I promise I'm going to come see you when I get back, okay?"

Angelica nodded, a huge smile across her face.

I stood up and faced Angel, who had just gotten her bag out of the trunk. I watched as she kissed Angelica, then told Rosario good-bye.

"Hey Angel," I cautiously said after Rosario had driven off.

"Hey," she responded.

There was a moment of awkward silence between us before I said, "So, are you excited about going to New Orleans?"

"Yeah." She didn't say anything else.

I was determined to make some headway. "Jasmine, Alexis, and Tameka are already here. They're inside helping Miss Rachel load up some stuff. Are you going to sit with us on the bus?"

Angel glanced over at Christina, who was standing near the bus glaring at us.

"Naw, I already told Christina I would sit with her."

"Angel . . ." I sighed.

"I gotta go," she said, without giving me time to finish.

My heart sank as I watched her dart off.

Christina had now moved over to a group of Hispanic guys and was pointing my way. *Great*, I thought, *just get everyone all worked up, why don't you?*

"What's up, cutie pie?"

I looked around; Vincent and another Gamma Man had just finished unloading their stuff from their car.

"Hey Vincent. Hey Julian."

Vincent noticed my uneasiness and glanced from me over to Christina and the others. "What's up?" he asked again.

I shook my head. "Nothing."

"Don't tell me 'nothing,'" Vincent said, continuing to look back and forth between us. "They're looking at you like you stole something."

"Yeah," Julian added, eyeing them as well. "If they're messin' with you, you just let us know. You're a Theta now. That means anybody messes with you, messes with us."

I couldn't help but note how that sounded exactly like something a Crip or a Blood would say.

"Naw, I'm straight," I lied.

"This wouldn't have anything to do with the rumors I heard that Christina and her crew were mad about Angel not making it, would it?" Vincent asked.

I sighed. I should've known this gossip would be all over school.

"I guess. But squash it. It's not even worth trippin' over."

"Naw, forget that," Julian said, stomping over toward Christina's group. Vincent followed and I groaned, then took off after them.

"Guys, it's nothing. Just leave it alone," I called out after them.

They ignored me and kept walking. "Yo, Hector," Vincent said as he approached the group. He was pointing at a tall guy who had stepped to the front of the crowd.

"Yo, the name is José. But you know that, *vato*. You're just trying to be funny," José said, clenching his fists.

"Hector, José, Jesus, whatever," Vincent said. "You got a beef with my girl, here?" He pointed at me.

"Naw, it seems your girl and her little friends got a beef with *my* girl," he replied, pointing at Angel. "Seems y'all got a problem with her people."

By this time, a small crowd had started to gather, including several of the Thetas.

"I think the problem is your girl just needs to start her own sorority and stay out of ours," Tori interjected. I should've known she'd throw in her two cents.

José flashed his palm in her face. "Was anybody talking to you? Go back to Africa or something."

Tori wiggled her neck. "No you didn't! I ain't from

Africa. I'm from the north side. Unlike your girl here," she said, pointing at Christina, "who probably snuck across the border last night."

Christina stepped up next to José. "For your information, I was born here. My mama was born here and my mama's mama was born here. Not that I need to explain anything to you." Her face was turning red with anger.

"Oh, but I'm sure that somebody snuck over on the fruit truck." Tori folded her arms across her chest and glared defiantly at Christina.

"Just like I'm sure your brother Ray-Ray is probably out carjacking someone right now," Christina retorted.

They were in each other's faces now and I just knew it was about to turn into an all-out brawl. Luckily, Miss Rachel came racing toward us.

"What is going on here?" she demanded.

Tori pointed her finger in Christina's face. "You'd better tell this *chica* I ain't the one. Don't get it twisted and think just because I'm pretty, I can't fight."

The next thing anyone knew, Christina swung at Tori, narrowly missing her face. Tori immediately lunged toward Christina, grabbing a handful of her hair, and the two began tussling.

It only took a few seconds for several chaperones to come over. They managed—although I don't know how—to break up the fight.

"Enough! This is insane," Rachel said after they got the

girls apart. "I can't believe you all are stooping to this level. You are young ladies, out here fighting like some common thugs!"

"I wasn't tryin' to fight, but I'm not gon' let her just hit me either!" Tori yelled.

"You need to learn to shut your face!" Christina screamed back.

"I said, stop it!" Rachel shouted. "I know this isn't a school-sponsored event, but this sort of behavior can still get you suspended!" She grabbed both of their arms and shook them. "So you both need to chill out!"

Both of them snatched their arms away, but they did calm down.

Rachel sighed heavily, then looked at Tori. "Do you know how long your ancestors fought to escape this ridiculous bigotry?" She then turned to Christina. "And yours fought just as hard to overcome prejudices, and here you all are fighting each other."

Rachel took a deep breath as the bus driver approached her.

"Mrs. Adams, if we're going to make it to New Orleans at a decent hour, we need to get loaded up and on the road," he said.

Rachel looked like she was thinking for a minute, then finally she said, "Jerome, I'm sorry. But under the circumstances, I just don't think it's a good idea for us to be taking a trip right now." She sighed and looked at us in disappointment. "They're supposed to be going to help people. Obviously, that's not a priority for them right now. No, as much as the people of New Orleans need us, we got some problems here at home that we need to take care of first," she said matter-of-factly.

Several people protested, but after the other chaperones backed Miss Rachel, I could see there was no changing their minds.

To say I was disappointed was an understatement, but deep down, I knew Miss Rachel was right. The trip had started off horribly before we even got out of the parking lot. We would've killed each other before the weekend was up. Yeah, we needed to get our own house in order before we went trying to straighten up someone else's.

24

Jasmine

I could tell Miss Rachel was still upset with us by the disgusted look on her face as me, Alexis, Camille, and Tameka silently piled into the room. Surprisingly, Angel walked in just as we had gotten settled. She didn't speak to us as she walked and sat a couple of rows over. I couldn't believe we were at the point where we weren't even talking to each other now. This whole mess was making me sick.

Miss Rachel took her usual spot at the oak podium at the front of the room. Her eyes were misty. "You know, I look at you girls sitting there with these horrible looks on your faces. The tension in this room is so thick you can cut it with two knives. I see all of this and it just breaks my heart. What happened to the girls who swore to me that they would be friends for life? What happened to the girls who made me so proud because they were role models for their peers? Huh?"

I wanted to let Miss Rachel know I didn't have anything

to do with any of this. Everything stemmed from everybody else's desire to be in a stupid sorority. I was perfectly fine with things just the way they were before.

"Have I been getting through to you all at all?" Rachel said, after no one said anything. She looked around at each of us.

I finally nodded before speaking up. "I hear everything you say, Miss Rachel. But obviously, I'm the only one. *I* know what it means to be a true friend," I stressed.

"Do you? Have you truly forgiven Alexis, or are you still harboring some anger yourself about the whole C. J. incident?" Rachel asked.

I folded my arms across my chest. "She's still breathing, so I must've forgiven her," I snapped.

Rachel shook her head as she turned to Angel. "Angel, you don't have anything to say? Ever since this foolishness started you've been missing in action, and when you are here, you don't add anything to the conversation."

Angel raised her left eyebrow. "I don't have anything to say."

Rachel sighed as she ran her fingers through her hair. "The sad part is that even if I get through to you all, it's not going to change what's going on at your school, in your community. It's not going to change this climate of hate that seems to be breeding." Rachel took a deep breath before continuing. "I'm sure you all have heard the saying, 'Love your neighbor.' Well, I wanted to remind you of one of my favorite Bible verses from Matthew 5:44. It says, 'Love your enemies and pray for those who persecute you.' "

"What is that supposed to mean?" Tameka asked, showing some interest for the first time since the meeting started.

"Loving your enemy is not as hard as it looks on the surface. It simply means respecting others and regarding their needs and desires as highly as we regard our own," Rachel answered.

"Yeah, right," I mumbled. "You have to give respect to get respect."

"Trust me," Rachel said. "I know how hard that can be better than anybody. Staying true to that thought is likely going to require the kind of assistance only God can provide. I mean, how can we learn to love people who treat us like dirt, especially when we don't even like them?"

She looked at me. I was hoping she didn't expect me to answer that because I was about to say, "You can't."

"Perhaps the secret is to recognize that that person, whoever they may be, is someone who is just as worthy of God's love as you or I," Rachel continued without waiting on me to answer.

After a few more minutes of her "love your neighbor" lecture, I heard her asking, "Does anyone have any suggestions on something we can do to improve this current situation? Not just among us, but in the community as a whole?"

The room was silent for a few minutes. Finally, I raised my hand. "What if you work with the school to put on a peace forum or something, you know, to promote unity." I don't know where the idea came from, but I just knew we had to do something.

Rachel looked at me and a small smile crept up on her face.

"Jasmine, that is a fantastic idea! The principal of Madison is a member here at Zion Hill. I'm going to give her a call and talk to her about that because I think that's something that everyone can benefit from right now. Don't you think that's a good idea?" She turned to Angel.

Angel shrugged. "Whatever."

I don't know if a peace forum was the answer, but watching Angel's nonchalant attitude, I knew we had to try something.

25

Camille

I really was starting to question just what I ever saw in Kalvin.

As usual, he was going on and on about how great of a football player he was, how he was probably going to skip college and go straight into the NFL. He was a good player, but I don't know if he was all that. He never gave me a chance to compliment him though because he was too busy complimenting himself and it was straight getting on my nerves.

"So did you catch me shaking off that dude that tried to tackle me at the game Saturday?" Kalvin said, as he brushed his fade for the ten thousandth time.

"Yes, Kalvin. I told you already, you were off the chain in that game," I replied in a monotone voice.

Kalvin and I were at the AMC Movie Theater near First Colony Mall, waiting to see this new movie starring Big Boi from Outkast. The previews were just starting and I found myself wishing the movie was over already.

"Yeah, yeah, I'm expecting the scouts to come knockin' down my door any day now," Kalvin continued. "I mean, I know I'm just a junior, but I'm so cold, they not gon' be able to wait."

I glanced over at Kalvin and wanted to throw up. I found myself wishing he would just shut up and sit there and look cute, since that's about all he had going for him.

I felt my phone vibrate and looked down to see that I had an incoming text message from Alexis. *How's it going?*

I didn't even try to be discreet. I just typed back, Horrible. This is the first and last date.

Alexis replied with: LOL. Call me when u get home and tell me everything.

"Who is that?" Kalvin asked, peering at my cell phone. "I know you ain't got no other dude textin' you while you chillin' with me."

I fought back a groan. "That wasn't another dude. That was my girl, Alexis. She was trying to see what I was getting into later," I lied.

Kalvin smiled. "Did you tell her you were busy because you were all into me?"

I just stared at him to see if he was serious. He was. I shook my head, leaned back, and turned my attention back to the movie screen.

Of course, it didn't faze Kalvin. He continued talking about himself, and I continued to tune him out. Kalvin rambled on for another five minutes, talking about what, I don't even know. But I did turn my attention back to him when I heard him snap, "Man, they make me sick."

"Who are you talking about?" I asked, looking around.

He pointed to a group of at least six Hispanic guys laughing and joking as they walked in the theater, up the stairs, and to the seats a couple of rows behind us.

"Dude, you got a problem?" one of the boys asked after Kalvin turned around and continued to stare at them.

Kalvin stood up. "You my problem," he loudly replied.

"What you say?" The boy stood and tried to make his way around his friend and back down the step. Kalvin stood up as well and poked out his chest.

"I didn't stutter."

I was just about to freak out when a Houston Police Department officer working security in the movie theater looked our way. "Don't start nothing," the officer called out. "Because I will take you to jail."

Both Kalvin and the other guy stood glaring at each other. I grabbed Kalvin's arm to pull him back down in the seat.

"Kalvin," I whispered. "What are you doing?"

"He'd better act like he knows," Kalvin huffed, his chest still puffed out.

The guy glanced at the police officer, who was standing at the bottom of the stairs, his hand planted firmly on the gun at his waist. Then the guy muttered something in

Spanish, his friends laughed, and they made their way on to their seats.

"Do you know them?" I asked after Kalvin finally sat back down.

"Naw." Kalvin said, still frowning.

A confused look crossed my face. "Then what are you talking about? Why do they make you sick?"

"They just taking over everything."

"What in the world does that mean?"

"I mean, haven't you heard?—they're the new minority, as my history teacher likes to say," Kalvin snapped.

"And? So what?" I replied.

"And that doesn't bother you?"

He was starting to sound just as crazy as Tori. "Why would it bother me? They've never done anything to me. And if one of them had, why would I have a beef with the whole race?"

Kalvin looked at me like I just wasn't getting it.

"So are you for real?" I continued, ignoring his stare. "You don't like Hispanics because you think they're taking over?"

"You doggone right," he said matter-of-factly. "You know they make up half the football team now, and two of them trying to steal my spot as quarterback. As if that would ever happen." He laughed.

It was my turn to stare at him crazy. "Football is competitive anyway. I mean, if it wasn't a Hispanic guy trying to take your spot, it would be somebody else, right? What difference does it make what they are? If anything, that should just make you want to work harder."

As the words came out of my mouth, I couldn't help but think about Angel. Why couldn't I have spoken up like that with the Thetas when it came to her?

"Boo, that's whack," Kalvin said, snapping me back to our conversation.

"What? The fact that I'm not prejudiced?"

"Call me what you want. I'm just tellin' it like it is." He leaned back and propped his feet up on the armrest of the chair in front of him, paying no attention to the people sitting there.

I was grateful when the opening credits began to play. I just wanted this movie to start and end. By this point, I think Kalvin was just as turned off by me as I was by him. Honestly, I didn't care. It was bad enough I had to deal with all that drama with Angel; I definitely didn't want to be dating a dude with jacked-up views just like Tori. If I'd been driving myself I probably would've just up and left.

As I watched Kalvin scowl once again at the group of Hispanic boys, I couldn't help but think Miss Rachel was right. There was a climate of hate brewing, and I had a bad feeling that it was about to spiral out of control.

26

Camille

$\mathcal{I}$ was so excited that Miss Rachel had agreed to let some of the AKAs and Deltas from Prairie View A&M come and visit our Good Girlz meetings. She actually thought it was a wonderful idea when Alexis presented it to her. She had decided she was hosting the community peace forum next week and had even gotten a couple other churches to join. So she thought the timing on this would be good.

All of us—with the exception of Angel—had gone out to eat yesterday and it had done a lot to ease the tension. We'd laughed and joked all evening. But convincing Angel to come to tonight's meeting had proven to be a bit of a challenge. After she had basically told us off for even setting this up, Alexis and I had decided that it would be best not to tell Angel what the meeting was about. There was no way she would have come if she had known what we had up our sleeve.

I was busy filling Alexis in on my disaster of a date last

night since I hadn't called her because my mom was trippin' that I'd left my room such a mess.

"I just saw a bunch of girls parking their cars," Tameka said, as she walked in. Angel was beside her. "What's going on at the church tonight? I didn't know there was another meeting here."

Angel mumbled a dry hello as she took a seat on the other side of the room. Just from the look on her face, I could tell she probably would've quit the group if she wasn't required to come to the Good Girlz meetings. After we got in trouble for shoplifting last year, the judge had made our Good Girlz meetings mandatory. Otherwise, I'm sure she would've bailed out.

Before anyone could answer Tameka, Miss Rachel walked in. "Our special guests are here, and they are ready whenever you girls are."

"What special guests?" Tameka asked with a confused look on her face.

"Didn't you girls know? We have a group of college women coming to talk to us tonight about sorority life," Miss Rachel said as she shot us a "shame on you" look.

"No, I had no idea." Angel looked at me and Alexis with daggers in her eyes.

"What are they talking to us for?" Tameka asked.

I didn't answer Tameka but I did want to try and explain to Angel why we hadn't told her. Only, I couldn't come up with the words to say. So I didn't say anything.

"Okay, ladies, I sense some tension in the room from some of you. Would any of you like to tell me what's going on before I invite our guests in?"

"Miss Rachel, everything is fine," I said. "Angel, why don't you come sit over here with us?"

She glared at me. "No, thanks. I'm fine right where I am."

Rachel shook her head. Before she exited the room she looked at all of us and said, "I'm not sure what the problem is since none of you are talking, but I expect all of you to be on your best behavior. I don't want to hear any arguing. Do I make myself clear? Jasmine?"

"What? I'm not saying anything," Jasmine replied.

When Rachel left the room, it was eerily quiet. Angel had a look of disgust on her face and Jasmine looked as if she were truly agitated and would rather be anywhere but in this room. Truthfully, I'd been against the idea at first, but now I was actually looking forward to it.

Rachel returned with several girls dressed in either Alpha Kappa Alpha or Delta Sigma Theta T-shirts. Crystal, Alexis's friend from high school, began.

"Ladies, thank you for inviting us to speak with you tonight. First, let me introduce my friends. These three lovely ladies are my sorors of Alpha Kappa Alpha Sorority, Inc." Three of the girls smiled and waved at us. Then she introduced the rest of the girls. "These other ladies are also good friends of mine and are members of Delta Sigma

Theta Sorority, Inc." Crystal paused. "We would like for this to be very casual and relaxed, so feel free to ask us anything and we will try to answer all your questions to the best of our ability."

Alexis didn't hesitate. "I have a question, Crystal. I have always heard that AKAs and Deltas don't like each other. But you all seem to be very close."

Crystal smiled and looked at her friends. "That is definitely a myth. First and foremost, we are all sisters in Christ. All of these ladies were very good friends of mine before we joined a sorority and they will always be my friends regardless of what group they belong to. You have to always remember that you make the sorority, the sorority shouldn't make you."

Angel coughed over in the corner. "So, even though you guys are different, you don't have any problems with each other?" Her voice was laced with attitude.

"Absolutely not. That's what makes our organizations so great. We're all different," an AKA said.

"I sure hope they're listening," Angel sarcastically mumbled. Then she shook her head and turned her attention to a spot on the wall.

Tameka raised her hand and asked, "Is one group better than the other?"

"Well, that depends on who you ask," a Delta jokingly replied. "But seriously, we all are founded on the same basic principles and that is serving our community. Regardless of whether you are Delta, AKA, Zeta, or Sigma Gamma Rho, we all strive to help those less fortunate than us. That's what it is all about."

"But what about sisterhood?" I asked. "Isn't that important?"

"Let me ask you a question," Crystal said. "Miss Rachel filled me in on your group and what you do. Camille, do you feel like all of the Good Girlz are your close friends?"

"Yes, they're more like the sisters I never I had."

"And Alexis, do you all depend on each other for love and support?"

"Sure, I don't know what I would do without them," Alexis replied.

"Well, that's what sisterhood is all about. You don't have to join a sorority to have a sisterhood. Just be a good friend, that's all it takes."

"Well, since all of you do the same thing, I think I want to be a Delta because I look good in red and white," Tameka announced.

"Sweetheart, I think you need to put a little more thought into your decision and do a little more research before you make that kind of decision," one of the Deltas said.

Angel spoke up from the corner. "I have a question. Do your sororities discriminate against other races becoming members?"

I cringed at that question and was a little ashamed to look in Angel's direction.

Crystal replied firmly. "No, we don't. Yes, the majority of our members are African American since we were founded by African Americans. However, we are open to anyone who wants to be a member. Both of our groups have a few Asian, Hispanic, and white members."

"Yeah," one of the AKAs agreed. "We recently had two Hispanic girls join at our school. I think it just depends on what or whom you can identify with."

Angel cut her eyes at us again. "Seems like you guys need to take this little meeting to the next Theta get-together," she said before leaning back in her seat.

After our guests wrapped up their presentations, Rachel thanked them and then turned to us. "Girls, I hope you got something from their presentation."

I nodded my head. I did. I think we all did. I just don't think it was what Miss Rachel had hoped we'd get.

27

Jasmine

I didn't have a good feeling. Don't ask me why, but I just knew this whole peace rally thing wasn't going to turn out like Miss Rachel hoped it would. Maybe it was the fact that Brentwood Park, where we were holding the rally in a tent, looked like something out of the 1960s. On one side there was a sea of black faces. On the other, nothing but Hispanics. The few white, Asian, and Indian students all sat safely in the back.

I called myself trying to make the first move toward togetherness, as Miss Rachel would say, and went to sit with Angel on the side with all of the Hispanic students. But before I could sit down good, Christina and her friends were looking at me all crazy. Of course, I ignored them.

"What are you doing?" Angel whispered as I slid into the empty seat next to her.

"What does it look like?" I responded. "I'm having a seat for the rally."

"Come on, Jaz. I don't want any trouble," Angel pleaded.

"Why would there be trouble?" I nonchalantly replied. Honestly, all the people staring at me were making me kinda nervous but I told myself, what could they really do in a place filled with security?

"Besides," I continued, "I didn't realize we had gone back to segregation."

Before Angel could respond, Christina and several other girls were standing over me.

"Yo, Angel, what's up with your girl? Why is she not over there with her own people?" she said.

I cocked my head and replied, "Last time I checked this was a free country and I could sit wherever I wanted to sit."

I didn't know why they were trippin' with me. I hadn't done anything to any of their skank behinds.

"It's all right," Angel nervously interjected. "Jasmine is cool."

"No, it ain't all right," Christina said. "She's one of them."

This was getting ridiculous. All this "them" and "us" stuff was making my head hurt.

"Miss Rodriguez, will you and your friends please take your seats. We're about to get the rally started." We all turned to look at the assistant principal, Mr. Hudson, who was trying to get everyone settled.

Christina rolled her eyes at me but she didn't say anything else. Lucky for her because I really didn't feel like putting out anyone's teeth today.

I looked over at Camille—who, of course, was sitting right in the middle of the Thetas. Alexis and Tameka were sitting right next to her. I hated that Camille and Alexis looked more and more like they were fitting right in with the Thetas every day. Camille also shot me a strange look when she noticed where I was sitting.

The program started with a brief presentation by the ROTC color guards from our school. Then we all stood and said the pledge of allegiance. After the senior class president welcomed everyone, there were a couple of poems read. One of them by this girl named Erin talked about unity. I was really feeling that one. I sure hoped Camille and Angel were listening.

Afterward, representatives from several campus and community organizations gave three-minute speeches. But when the junior class president, a cute dark-skinned black guy, got up to speak, someone from the row behind me shouted, "Put some Vaseline on those ashy lips!"

I immediately turned around, only to find several Hispanic boys cracking up. I didn't have to say anything to him though because the next thing I knew, several guys from the football team were surrounding him. Kalvin, the guy Camille had gone out with, was leading the pack.

"Yo, which one of you punks said that?" Kalvin said.

"Yo' mama," someone yelled from a couple of rows over.

The football players looked around to see who was doing the shouting.

Then a chair flew past me and into the head of the guy sitting behind me. Before anyone could blink, it was on. The next thing I knew, all those guys were going at it. Several people started screaming as they scurried out of the way. I hit the floor, grabbing Angel and pulling her down as well.

"Let's get out of here!" I shouted, crawling away. People were fighting, swinging wildly, and jumping over seats attacking each other.

"Call the police!" someone screamed.

I got to the edge of the row, but it was so chaotic, I couldn't see what happened to Angel. I stood and tried to look around for her, but this tall lanky boy knocked me to the ground trying to climb over the chairs past me. I looked up just in time to see security racing from the other side of the park. They immediately started grabbing the people who were fighting the most. I stumbled to the front, trying to escape the madhouse.

"Jasmine, Jasmine!" I heard Camille calling my name.

"I'm right here." I pushed my way through the crowd to her and began looking around at the chaos. "Where's Alexis?"

"I don't know." We both looked around for a minute.

"There she is," Camille said as Alexis came limping toward us.

"Oh my God. Do you see this? They broke the straps. Do you know how much this Louis Vuitton costs?" Alexis wailed as she held up her multicolored purse.

Leave it to Alexis. All kinds of madness was breaking out around us, and she's worried about her stupid purse!

"Where's Angel?" Camille said.

I shrugged. "She was right behind me. But I lost her."

"Oh my God," Alexis cried again as a cop tackled one of the football players to the ground. "We need to get out of here."

Just then we heard a bloodcurdling scream. Everyone turned toward where the noise was coming from. "She's bleeding! She's bleeding!" someone shrieked.

We probably should've taken off, but we raced over toward where the scream came from. I stopped dead in my tracks. I saw Angel's black tennis shoes and her army pants before I saw her. I struggled to catch my breath as I slowly made my way through the crowd. Angel was lying on the ground, blood pooling underneath her. She was crying as she struggled to catch her breath. I immediately shook off my shock and raced to her side. Camille was right behind me.

"Oh my God! Angel! What happened?" Camille asked.

"Some . . . somebody stabbed me."

"Oh my God, oh my God. Somebody call an ambulance," I cried.

"They're on their way," someone behind me answered.

"Put some pressure on it," I heard another person yell.

"Camille, please, please don't let me die," Angel said as she grabbed Camille's hand.

By this time, Camille was crying as well. Me and Alexis were leaning down by Angel. Tears were streaming down Angel's cheeks. "D-don't let me die. Angelica needs me. I'm sorry, I d-didn't mean to be a jerk."

"Angel, just be quiet. Hang on. Help is on the way," I said.

The fight had finally been broken up, although there was still all kinds of chaos around the park. I felt a sense of relief as the wail of the sirens grew louder. I knew this whole race thing had gotten out of control, but I never would've imagined that it would result in something like this.

28

Camille

If Angel didn't recover, I'd never forgive myself. I grabbed a pillow off my full-size bed and put it over my head. I was all cried out, but I still couldn't help but feel like my world was falling apart.

I had been too depressed to do anything all day long and stayed holed up in my room. My mother had checked on me periodically, and I know I was starting to worry her.

Sure enough, she poked her head in my room again. "Camille, do you want to talk about it?" she asked.

At first, I was going to tell her no, but I really did want to get some things off my chest, and a lot of it had to do with the Thetas. And since my mother was in a sorority, maybe she'd understand.

"I guess," I mumbled.

"Is this about Angel?" she asked as she sat down on the bed next to me. I nodded.

"How is she doing?"

I moved the pillow and flipped over. "She's doing a lot better." We'd stayed with Angel at the hospital all day yesterday. We finally left after her mother asked that we all go home and get some rest. The only reason I could bring myself to leave was because the doctor told us Angel was out of danger. The knife hadn't touched any major organs.

"So, are you ready to tell me what's going on with you guys?" My mother stroked my hair, and the tears I thought I no longer had started to flow again.

"Mama, this is all my fault," I cried as I buried my head in her lap. I sobbed for a couple of minutes, then sat up and sniffed. "Trying out for the Theta Ladies was all my idea. I never meant for it to come to this: Angel getting hurt, us barely speaking. I just wanted to be a Theta."

My mother wiped away my tears and took my hands. Even though she could nag the heck out of me sometimes, for the most part, my mom and I had a good relationship. Ever since she almost died from a heart attack last year, things had gotten a lot better between us and I'd really come to value her opinion.

"Everything happens for a reason, dumplin', so maybe now is not the time for you to be joining a sorority. Maybe you should save that for college because it's obvious these girls aren't mature enough to understand the real meaning behind sororities. Unfortunately, from what you've told me, the Thetas are led by a girl who goes against everything sororities are all about, be it on the college level or in high school. They're about sisterhood, and sometimes that sister may not look just like you." She sighed as she dropped my hand.

"You young people don't know the things our people have had to endure. If you did, you would see how detrimental hate is." She lifted my chin. "Let me tell you something we don't talk about much in our family. It's too painful for your grandmother to even think about."

My grandmother lived in a senior citizens' center about twenty minutes away. Over the years she had shared a lot of stories with me, so I couldn't imagine that there was something she had never told me.

"You've heard us talk about your grandfather, right?" It seemed like my mother was forcing herself to tell me whatever she was trying to tell me. Her eyebrows furrowed and she had stress lines all across her face.

I nodded. "Yeah, Grandpa died when you were just a little girl."

"That's right. But we never talked about how he died." She took a deep breath. "He was lynched."

"You mean like hung?" I asked in disbelief.

My mother solemnly nodded. "He was very active in Mississippi, trying to help get black people registered to vote. A lot of white people in town didn't like that."

I was stunned. I was also having trouble figuring out

how this story was supposed to bolster my mother's case that we should all just get along. If my grandfather was killed because of the color of his skin, she was entitled to have a racist attitude. Wasn't she?

"Daddy was with me and Mama at the store picking up a few groceries one day when we were approached by several white men," she began. "I couldn't have been any more than three. But I remember them yelling at my daddy. Mama was crying and shielding me behind her back. The next thing I knew, those men were dragging both of my parents to a field. They strung Daddy up right there on a big old oak tree and they were about to do the same to Mama."

I stared at my mother, my eyes wide in shock. "Oh, my God. B-but you're so nice to *everybody*. If anyone has a reason to hate someone because of their color, it's you."

My mother closed her eyes and sighed like I just didn't get it. "They could've killed Mama, too. And maybe even me. But do you know what stopped them?"

I didn't have an answer, so I just shook my head.

"Another white man who just so happened to be passing by," she continued. "He didn't know us from Adam, but he came over and pleaded for my mother's life. He knew they could've easily killed him as well, but he begged them to let us go. So how can I hate white people when it was a white person who saved me and my mother's lives?"

This whole story was too much. And I still wasn't seeing

what it had to do with anything. "But this isn't between blacks and whites. It's the Hispanic and black kids who are mad at each other."

"Don't you see it's the same thing? It's hate. Pure and simple. You're judging someone based on their race." She let out a long sigh. "That man who saved our lives helped us out tremendously after Daddy died. Daddy took care of everything, and Mama didn't work so it was really hard on us after he died. But Charles Stamps gave us money to move, to start over and basically rebuild our lives. Imagine if he had just said, 'Oh, they're black, I won't help them.' We would've been in a world of trouble. He didn't see color. And I've tried to live my life the same way."

I now understood where my mother was coming from. She had a valid point. Until this whole Theta thing, I never really saw color or race. I still didn't, really. But I'd aligned myself with people who did.

I hugged my mother and thanked her for helping open my eyes. I knew now exactly what I needed to do.

29

Camille

Everything felt so surreal as I walked up to the hospital doors. The last time I had been in this place was when my mom was rushed here after having a heart attack. Just like then, I felt like this was all my fault.

Alexis and Jasmine, who were with me, read my mind.

"Camille, you know this is not your fault, right?" Alexis said to me.

Jasmine nodded in agreement. "Something like this was bound to happen with everything that was going on."

I wiped at the tears that had started trickling down my cheeks. "That's what I keep trying to tell myself, but why did it have to be one of *my* best friends who got stabbed?" I said as we walked up to Angel's hospital room. "This whole peace forum was supposed to promote unity and it just ended horribly."

Before anyone could respond, Christina came barreling down the hallway, jumped in front of the doorway, and blocked the entrance to Angel's room.

"What are y'all doing here? I can't believe you have the nerve to show your face at this hospital. This is all your fault anyway. Angel wouldn't be in here if you were her real friends!" she spat. "But don't worry, you can go back to your precious little sorority sisters. Angel's family and true friends have this under control."

Jasmine, whose face was turning red, exploded. "What? How you gon' tell us we aren't her real friends? Were you there when Angel ran away from home and had nowhere to go? Were you there when we had to drive all the way to Victoria, Texas, to drag her back to Houston? How about when that triflin' baby daddy of hers refused to help take care of Angelica? Or better yet, were you there when Angel went into labor and had to have the baby all by herself? Uhh, no, I don't think you were, because *we were* there. So don't talk to me about being a true friend!"

Jasmine was yelling so loudly that a nurse at the nearby station cleared her throat and shot us dirty looks. Jasmine lowered her voice. "You just came on the scene a month ago and all of a sudden you've made yourself Angel's personal bodyguard," she continued. "Girl, please, you better move out of my way and let me in this room."

Angel's sister, Rosario, must've heard the commotion in the hallway. She came bustling out of the room to see what the problem was.

"Excuse me, ladies, but my sister did just get stabbed. Can y'all keep that nonsense away from her door? She does not need that kind of stress." Rosario's eyes were puffy, and I'd never seen her angry.

"I'm sorry, Rosario," I said. "We just wanted to check on Angel, and Christina won't move out of the way. We promise no more arguing, okay?"

Rosario looked at us skeptically. "Okay, but my mom is upset enough as it is. Don't come up in here with that drama, upsetting her even more."

We all nodded. Jasmine cut her eyes at Christina, who reluctantly moved out of the way.

We opened the door just in time to hear the doctor say that Angel was going to be okay. The knife had just missed her kidney. A couple more inches and she would have died before she even made it to the hospital.

Angel lay in bed, pale as a ghost. There were all kinds of tubes connected to her arms. Angel's mom was sitting on the side of the bed, holding her daughter's hand. She looked like she would collapse from exhaustion at any given moment.

"Thank you, Doctor. I'm so glad she's going to be okay," Mrs. Lopez said.

He gave her a reassuring nod. "You're a lucky mother," he said, glancing at his chart. "And luckily, you have a fighter on your hands. Well, I have to make my rounds. Buzz your nurse if you need anything."

Mrs. Lopez stood as the doctor left the room. "Oh, hi, girls," she said, finally noticing us. "Angel is going to be so happy that you came to check on her. She's still a little groggy, but I'm sure she will be excited that you all came."

Angel's mom obviously had no idea that we had barely been speaking to Angel. Jasmine gave Christina a "now what" look and Christina scowled back at her as Mrs. Lopez turned back to Angel and began gently stroking her hair.

"Sweetie, your friends are here to see you. Your sister and I are going to go down to the cafeteria and get some coffee so you and your friends can have some privacy. We'll be back in a little bit.

"Oh, and girls?" her mom said to us before exiting the room. "Thank you for always being there for *mija*. It makes me feel better knowing that she has such good friends in her corner."

I now officially felt like the scum of the earth. Alexis must have been feeling the same way because she put her head down and said, "There's no need to thank us, Mrs. Lopez."

"Yeah, really you shouldn't," Christina snidely remarked from the corner.

Angel, who hadn't said anything since we entered the room, softly spoke. "Christina, can you please give us a minute? I think we need to talk."

Christina let out a nasty sigh and reluctantly followed Angel's mom and sister out of the room.

For what seemed like forever, there was a silence that blanketed the room as we looked from one to the other.

"Okay, I guess I'll start," I said before I lost my nerve. "Angel, you know we never meant for this to happen. If I had known things would end up like this, I would've never asked any of you guys to join the Thetas. And then with the peace forum, we were only trying to help the situation, and instead I think we made it worse. You know we all love you regardless of what sorority we may belong to. We were friends long before the Thetas came along and we will be friends long after they are gone. It doesn't matter . . ." My eyes were starting to tear up and I felt a lump forming in my throat as I tried to continue. "It doesn't matter . . ."

"I think what the crybaby is trying to say," Jasmine interrupted, "is that it doesn't matter to us if you are black, Spanish, or white with purple polka dots, we are always going to be there for you."

"Leave it to you, Jasmine, to always lighten the mood," Angel said as she smiled at us. "Look y'all, I know I have been acting a little strange lately, but my feelings were really hurt when I found out the real reason I didn't get picked for the Thetas. I just thought it would be best if I started hanging with some friends more like me." Angel winced in pain.

"Save your strength," Alexis told her. "You don't have to explain anything to us. I think we've all said and did some things we aren't proud of. So I think it's safe to say that we are all sorry." By this point me, Alexis, and Angel were in tears. Even Jasmine was a little misty-eyed, although you could tell she was fighting back her tears.

"We have been through so much within the past year and a half, and we've become such close friends," I said. "I just hate that it had to come to this in order for us to realize nothing is worth jeopardizing that friendship."

Angel reached out for my hand. "Nothing at all."

We turned when we heard a noise at the door. Miss Rachel stood in the doorway with a huge smile on her face. "I knew you girls would make me proud," she said, walking in the room. "Angel, how are you feeling, sweetie?"

Angel stretched her other hand out for Alexis, who took it. "Miss Rachel, I'm sorry. And just so you know, I'm feeling better now." She squeezed both of our hands. "Much, much better now that my friends are here."

30

Camille

"So, how's your little *chica*?" Tori snidely remarked. She was so working my nerves. Angel had almost died behind this foolishness and she was still trippin'.

Lynn stood next to her, looking uneasy. "Tori, chill out," she said.

I ignored Tori as I threw my books in my locker and slammed the door shut.

"Dang, I'm just asking," Tori said, rolling her eyes. "Can't I be concerned?"

"Don't act like you care what happens to Angel," I snapped.

We were standing in the hallway about to go to lunch. Even though it had been three days and Angel was doing much better, she was still in the hospital. Me, Jasmine, and Alexis had been up to see her daily.

Today was our first day back to school since the rally. Monday and Tuesday had been teacher in-service days. I'd already told myself that I wouldn't be sitting with the Thetas today and was actually looking forward to a nice, quiet lunch with Jasmine.

"You know, Tori, not that you really care, but Angel almost died," I said.

"*And?* It's not like I'm the one that stabbed her."

"Yeah, but this whole climate that you're creating, making people hate each other because of their race . . . It's just crazy."

Tori sucked her teeth like I was getting on her nerves. "Look, you and Alexis need to decide who you're with. Us, your sisters, or some Mexican from the other side of the tracks."

I looked at her in utter disgust. It's like I was seeing her in a whole different light. I mean, I knew she could act ugly, but right now, she *was* ugly.

"You know, I can't understand what I ever saw in the Theta Ladies," I finally said. "Especially if you're representative of what and who they really are. I went to bat for this organization every time someone talked junk about you. But I believed in what you all were doing." I sighed when it was obvious I wasn't getting through to her. "You know, my grandfather was killed because of the color of his skin."

"Wahhhh, wahhh, wahhh," Tori sang. "Break out the tissue. Am I supposed to be moved by that?"

I looked at her and shook my head. "You know, it

doesn't surprise me that you're not." I quickly removed my pink-and-white T-shirt, revealing the white tank top I wore underneath. "Consider me out of the Theta Ladies." I tossed the T-shirt in her face.

I started walking down the hall. Tori called out after me, "Don't come crying back to us when you figure out who your real friends are!"

I just threw up my hand as I continued to walk away. I probably should've tried to hang around and let Jasmine know I was leaving, but I was so disgusted, I didn't even want to be in the same building with the Theta Ladies.

I could barely concentrate through the rest of my classes. Not because I was upset about the Thetas. Truthfully, I couldn't care less about them now. I just couldn't get my mind off Angel. I said another quick prayer, thanking God that she was going to be all right and that our friendship wasn't broken permanently.

"I heard about what you told the Thetas earlier."

I looked up to see Jasmine standing over my desk. I had been in such a daze, that I hadn't even realized it was fifth-period English, a class I shared with Jasmine.

"That was less than two hours ago. How'd you hear about it?"

"Girl, you know gossip spreads around here faster than the flu." She sat down in the seat next to me. "So you finally saw their true colors, huh?"

I cut my eyes at Jasmine. I really wasn't in the mood for

an "I told you so" speech. She must've known that because she left it alone.

I sighed. "You know it's just a lot of things I wanted to do with the Thetas. I really liked what they were about. And not just the stepping." I added, smiling at Jasmine.

She shrugged. "Whatever you say."

"But I definitely can't get with this. I mean, Angel almost died, and I feel like we're partly responsible."

Jasmine looked at me like she wanted to say, "You were." I was grateful when she didn't say anything.

"Are you going by the hospital?" I asked her.

"Yeah. I sent a text for Alexis to pick me up."

"A text? When did you get a cell phone?"

"Girl, please. I used C. J.'s." She held up a blue T-Mobile Sidekick.

I grinned widely. "C. J.'s, huh? So I guess we're back together now?"

"Naw, it ain't even all that. We're just friends." She shrugged, but I could tell she was trying to play it down.

"You know you need to give that boy another chance. I mean, you are using his phone."

"Whatever," Jasmine said. "I just used his phone, that's all. We're not getting married."

"Cell phone today, a ring tomorrow, because you know you want to forgive him."

Jasmine rolled her eyes.

"I told you. Jasmine and C. J. sitting in a tree . . ." I began singing.

"Oh, my God, please do not start that elementary stuff."

"K-I-S-S-I-N-G."

"Don't make me get up and move."

"First comes love . . ." I continued.

"Then comes Jasmine with these two duckies upside your head," she replied, holding up her fists.

I stopped messing with her and laughed. It was a refreshing laugh, one that had me more sure than ever that the Good Girlz were finally back on the right track.

31

Camille

"Hey, Camille. Can we talk to you for a minute?"

I turned toward the voice shouting to me from down the hall.

I saw Lynn and quickly scanned the faces of the five girls with her. I was looking for Tori because if she was with them, I was leaving. I didn't have anything to say to her. She wasn't, so I stood and waited for them to catch up with me. Even though Lynn, Raquelle, and the others had never stood up to Tori, they really hadn't been that bad; I didn't have a beef with them.

I watched as they approached me. Tameka was right in the center like she'd been a Theta all her life.

"Look, we just want to say we're sorry for what happened to Angel," Lynn started. She looked really sincere, but that didn't change the facts, so I didn't let myself be moved by her words.

"Are you really?"

Lynn sighed as she looked at the other girls. "I know Tori can be a super jerk sometimes and we probably let her get away with way more than we should."

"You think?"

"But the bottom line is," Lynn continued, "we got to talking and we believe in what we do with the Theta Ladies. This is a great organization, and we hate the cloud that's hanging over us. We finally had to tell ourselves that a lot of that is coming from Tori."

I nodded in agreement. "Ain't that the truth."

It was Raquelle's turn to speak up. "We're saying all of this to say that we plan to take a vote and remove Tori from office as president."

I sucked my teeth skeptically. "Yeah, right. Like she will ever go for that."

A determined look crossed Lynn's face. "Well, according to the rules of our organization, she doesn't have much choice. If the majority of us want her out, she has to go. And we want her out."

Tameka finally spoke up. "I told you the Thetas are more than just about Tori. We wanted to be a part of the organization for a reason and we shouldn't let Tori take that from us."

I couldn't help but stare at Tameka. She hadn't even asked about Angel, nor had she bothered to come by the hospital and visit her.

Raquelle held my Theta T-shirt out to me. "We would

like you to remain a member of the Theta Ladies and help us to do the things we were actually formed to do."

I looked at Raquelle, then at Lynn. I wanted to believe them. Honestly, I did believe them. But even still, I just wasn't feeling the Thetas anymore.

"You know what, no thanks. Right now, my concentration is just on my friend. My true friend, Angel. I wish you all the best." I turned and walked away.

"Camille," Tameka yelled.

I stopped and spun around. "What, Tameka?"

"Are you for real?" She looked at me in shock. "You're just gon' throw everything away?"

"Everything like what?" I shifted my weight as I waited to see how she was going to try and even fix her lips to convince me to stay with the Thetas.

"Being a Theta."

I looked at Tameka proudly wearing her Theta Lady jacket and couldn't do anything but shake my head in disgust. "You don't feel the least bit bad about everything that's gone down?" I asked, trying to reason with her.

She looked around nervously, like she really didn't want anyone to hear her answer. "You know I feel bad about what happened to Angel," she said, stepping closer to me. "But come on, it's not like it's Tori's fault."

I just stared at Tameka. She couldn't really be that dumb. "Do you really believe that, Tameka? I mean, you saw how the blacks and Hispanics were going at it. Do you really think them rejecting Angel had nothing to do with that?"

Tameka rolled her eyes. "Please, Camille. The blacks and Hispanics have been going at it for the past year. So don't blame it on the Thetas."

"Maybe so. But we just gave them even more reason to hate each other." I sighed, trying to figure out why I was even bothering. Tameka wasn't trying to hear nothing bad about the Thetas.

"So, you're out? Just like that."

"I'm out. Just like that."

"What about Alexis?"

"She feels the same way." Alexis hadn't said point blank that she was quitting the Thetas, but last night she alluded how this was not what she bargained for at all. I knew I wouldn't have to do much convincing to get her to leave the Thetas as well.

I knew there was nothing I could say to Tameka to get her to open her eyes. That was fine with me. If she wanted to be blind, so be it. Me, I was through. The Thetas had almost caused me to lose my best friend. Now, my only focus was getting that friendship back.

32

Jasmine

The door creaked as Camille stuck her head in Angel's hospital room. I was sitting beside the bed reading her an article in *Essence* magazine about Usher.

"Hey, Jasmine," Camille softly said. "Do you think it's okay for me and Alexis to come in?"

I looked up at Camille. She was standing in the doorway looking kinda pathetic if you asked me, like she hadn't had any sleep in days. Alexis, who was standing behind her, didn't look too hot either.

"Come on in," I said. "Angel is knocked out. They got her all doped up. Her mom went with Miss Rachel to fill out some paperwork."

Alexis and Camille eased into the room, never taking their eyes off of Angel. I know they were hurt to see her lying there with tubes stuck all in her body. Her once colorful skin was now a pasty shade. She was lying back on a mountain of pillows, her eyes closed.

"How is she doing?" Alexis asked. "I thought they said she was gonna be okay."

"She is," I replied. "Her mom said it looks a lot worse than it is and that she'll probably be able to go home at the end of the week. She just has to get her strength back up. She's been asleep the whole time I've been here." I looked at my watch. "Which has been about twenty minutes."

"Were you reading to her?" Camille asked, pointing to the magazine.

I quickly pushed the magazine behind my back. "Oh, that's nothing. I was just reading out loud."

"Awww, you *were* reading to her," Alexis said. "I heard you talking about Usher. You know how much she loves Usher so you decided to read to her. That is so sweet."

"Whatever." I tossed the *Essence* down. I didn't want them to think I was getting all soft and stuff.

Alexis stepped closer to me and rubbed my arm. "Come on, Jazzy, admit it. You were doing something sweet."

I snatched my arm away. "I told you I was just reading out loud. What's the big deal? And stop calling me Jazzy."

"The big deal is you try to act all hard, but you really have a heart of gold deep down. I think you're the sweetest one of the group." Alexis grinned widely.

"Isn't she though?" Camille added.

"Man, go on somewhere with that," I snapped, waving them off.

"So you guys can't even stop fighting while I'm lying here dying." We all turned toward Angel, who had opened her eyes and now wore a small smile.

"Angel," Camille said, going to her side. "You are not dying."

"Well, I gotta milk this for all it's worth," Angel joked. "It's not often I can have my friends cater to me hand and foot."

"How are you feeling?" Camille asked after our laughter died down.

"Like I've been stabbed," Angel responded. She winced as she shifted and tried to get comfortable. "But, the good news is the doctor said I should be able to go home in a couple of days."

"Yeah, Jasmine told us," Alexis said. "That is so wonderful."

"Yeah, tell me about it." Angel looked back and forth between the three of us. "What were you guys arguing about?"

Alexis smiled. "We weren't arguing. I was just complimenting Jasmine for sitting here and reading to you."

Angel tried to sit up, but then she grimaced again and fell back against the pillow.

"Isn't it sweet?" Alexis asked.

"Jasmine was reading to me?" Angel said, as she looked at me in disbelief. "Wow, you must've thought I was a goner for sure."

"Would you all shut up," I said, rolling my eyes. "It's not that big of a deal."

"Really it is." Camille added, "Since you just learned how to read yesterday."

"Okay, Martin Lawrence. Enough with the jokes already."

We all laughed for a minute before Camille said, "I heard that the police know who stabbed you."

"They do? Who is it?" Angel asked, her tone turning serious.

Camille shook her head in disgust. "Some boy that doesn't even go to our school. He's a dropout. He just wanted to get in on a fight."

"Why would he stab me?" Angel asked.

"He wasn't trying to stab you specifically. You just got caught in the middle as he was going after someone he had a beef with earlier."

I looked at Camille in disbelief. "So you mean this wasn't even about race?"

"Naw. He got into it with another guy over a stereo. He just used the fight at the peace forum to settle the score," Camille replied.

"That's jacked up," I said.

"Wow." Angel looked down at her bandaged side. "I know one thing. This was so not worth it."

Camille walked over and gently touched Angel's arm. "Angel, I can't say it enough. I'm really sorry about all of this."

Angel smiled as she squeezed Camille's hand. "I'm sorry, too. And it's not your fault. Shoot, I'm just as much to blame. I don't even like Christina and those guys. I just started hanging around them because we're all Spanish, so I thought they were just like me. But I found out I have absolutely nothing in common with them."

"*We're* just like you," I said. "Well, Alexis is too rich to be just like us but we love her anyway."

Alexis playfully swatted at my arm. "You're just hatin'. Angel knows the deal, pickle."

We all stopped and looked at her.

She was cheesing like crazy. "Get it? Dill pickle. Like sour pickle."

I didn't take my eyes off of her. "If you ever, ever, ever, ever, say some corny stuff like that again, I will hit you in your jaw," I said.

We all busted out laughing.

"Guys," Angel asked as the laughter died down. "Are we straight?"

"We're straight," Camille said with a smile.

"And we're gon' stay straight," I added.

"We're as straight as my hair after a perm," Alexis said.

Again, we all looked at her.

"You have got to be the corniest person I've ever met," I said.

"But you love me anyway." Alexis grinned.

I returned her grin. That I did. I loved them all and I was so grateful that the Good Girlz were friends again. And this time I was determined that nothing would come between us ever again.

Reading Group Guide for
Fair-Weather Friends
by ReShonda Tate Billingsley

Description

The Good Girlz of Zion Hill are back for new adventures and, of course, plenty of drama. When Camille sees her high school's Theta sorority performing a spectacular step show, she decides that she and her friends must become Thetas at any cost. Camille talks Angel, Alexis, and Jasmine into joining with her, but problems arise when Jasmine won't take part in the grueling hazing rituals led by Tori, Theta president and Jasmine's longtime enemy. When Jasmine learns a nasty secret about Tori, she knows that she has to step in before her friends make a terrible mistake. With the help of First Lady Rachel Jackson Adams, Jasmine fights to keep her friends together, as the Thetas and racial problems at school threaten to tear the Good Girlz apart.

Questions for Discussion

1. *Fair-Weather Friends* is the fifth book in Billingsley's Good Girlz series. How have the Good Girlz changed from earlier books? Who has matured the most? Who seems to have changed least?

2. Who is your favorite member of the Good Girlz? Have your opinions of any of the characters changed from book to book?

3. From the moment Camille sees the Thetas performing, she wants to be a part of their world. "I couldn't stop talking about the Theta Ladies. As a matter of fact, the whole school was talking about them." Why is Camille so drawn to the Thetas? Why does it take her so long to see the downside of the Thetas, even after the issues that come up with Angel?

4. How does each character's past shape the decisions she makes? How do they all learn from the mistakes of others?

5. Why does Jasmine see through the Thetas much earlier than her friends do? How is she different from the rest of the Good Girlz?

6. What does this book tell us about race relations? Have you or people you know experienced racism or other prejudices? How do you react to people who are outwardly prejudiced?

7. Rachel tells Jasmine, "I want you to understand that friends go through their ups and downs all the time . . . Keep trying to get through to them. Come up with a plan. Anything. Just don't give up on your friendship." Have any of your friendships been tested? How did you handle it? How do you work to maintain your friendships?

8. Do you think Tori's racial views reflect those of many people? Why do you think people like Tori act the way they do?

9. What does the book tell us about the nature of groups and

exclusivity? Discuss the ways in which organized groups can positively and negatively impact society.

10. What were some of the funniest parts of the book? The most shocking? What were some other lines and scenes that stood out?

11. Who are some of your other favorite motivational fiction writers?

Activities to Enhance Your Book Club

1. This novel talks about the importance of community service. Get your group together for a volunteer outing. Take a look at http://www.networkforgood.org/volunteer/ or http://www.redcross.org/donate/volunteer/ for ideas. Or, brainstorm ideas for activities that support your favorite causes.

2. Have a dinner party where everyone prepares a favorite fun and easy dish. Bring music to play while you cook so you can share both songs and recipes. Try http://www.foodnetwork.com if you need ideas.

3. Get to know one another better. Write questions such as "What is your favorite book of all time?" and "Which fictional character do you most identify with?" on slips of paper. Drop them in a hat and pass them around.

4. Learn more about ReShonda Tate Billingsley and her upcoming books at http://www.myspace.com/goodgirlz1 and http://www.reshondatatebillingsley.com.

Don't miss the next

Good Girlz adventure!

FRIENDS 'TIL
THE END

Coming in February 2009

Turn the page for a sneak peek. . . .

Jasmine

"You so stupid you have to put lipstick on your head just to make up your mind."

I looked over at my brother and laughed. "You so stupid you tried to put M&Ms in alphabetical order."

"You so fat, I tried to drive around you and ran out of gas," he said.

"You so corny, you should be in a field."

He looked at me, paused, then busted out laughing. "Okay, now *that* was corny."

"It was, wasn't it?" I admitted. I guess I'd been hanging around Alexis too long, because she was known for her corny comments.

I actually couldn't believe how much fun Jaquan and I were having just walking and talking. My grandmother had sent me to the corner store to get some cooking oil so she could finish frying chicken for dinner. Out of the blue, Jaquan had offered to walk with me, which definitely caught me off guard because my brother didn't *offer* to do anything. When I tried to ask him what was up, he made like he wanted to buy himself some candy from the store. But I had seen two bags of Skittles in his backpack earlier. Even so, I let it slide. I just figured we were finally getting to the point where we enjoyed each other's company.

"So, what did the coach say about you being a McDonald's All American?" I asked. I was so proud of Jaquan. Only three boys in the whole city of Houston had made it on the national McDonald's All American basketball team and my brother was one of them. He was blowing people away with his skills on the basketball court. He knew he was good, but that didn't stop him from getting out there and practicing every single day, and I think it was definitely only making him better.

"Coach said I'm gonna have Division One colleges beating down my door."

My eyes widened. This was the first time my brother had ever mentioned college, at least with so much enthusiasm.

"I know I have two more years but I'm tellin' you, if I have a shot at getting out of this dump"—he motioned around the neighborhood—"then I'm takin' it. Plus, get this, Coach even said I shouldn't be surprised if the pro scouts start looking at me."

I stopped and turned to him. "What?"

"I know, I know. Everybody in the neighborhood thinks they can go pro but I'm not bankin' on that. Yeah, I'd love to and yeah, I think I'm good enough to make it, but honestly, I'm just trying to get a college degree so I can get a good job, then get us all out of this neighborhood. It's gettin' rougher by the day. By the time Jaheim and Jalen get to high school, it's gon' be nothin' but trouble on every corner. The streets are rough."

His suddenly serious tone was catching me off guard. Now that I thought about it, lately he'd been having more and more moments like this, when he would all of a sudden turn serious. Maybe it was just all part of him growing up.

We made our way inside the store and I picked up the cooking grease and a loaf of bread. I smiled inside as I noted the fact that Jaquan didn't buy any candy. He just stood around as I paid for my stuff. We exited the store, and I was just about to call him on it when four boys in baggy pants passed by us. They were cursing, laughing, and talking loud.

The expression on Jaquan's face changed when he spotted them.

"Well, if it isn't Jaquan Jones," the short, stocky one in the front said. All four of the boys stopped in front of us on the sidewalk.

"What's up?" Jaquan said unenthusiastically.

"Same ol', same ol'." The guy stroked his chin. "I thought I told you to get wit' me."

"I've been a little busy," Jaquan replied. His whole body

looked tense. "I'm just tryin' to stay focused on playing ball."

The guy threw up his hands. "Hey, I'm not a difficult brotha. I can respect that. But I also think you can show us a little love, too."

"You don't need my love, Tonio. Looks like you got plenty of it," Jaquan said, motioning to the boys behind him.

These guys were freaking me out. All of them looked shady. Two of them wore hoodies and they all looked like they'd just been dropped off by the prison truck. When I looked at the two teardrops on Tonio's face, I knew that wasn't a good sign.

"Yo, man. I'm gonna be looking to hear from you," Tonio said.

"Yeah, whatever," Jaquan replied.

"Hey, foxy mama," Tonio said, turning his attention to me. He licked his lips as he looked me up and down like I was a pork chop sandwich.

"Umm, is this 1975? *Foxy mama*? Are you for real?" I asked.

He stepped in my face. He barely came to my chin. "Get with me and I'll show you how real I am."

I took two steps backward. "Get out of my face before I show you how real *I* am."

Jaquan rested his hand on my lower arm. "Jasmine, chill."

Tonio broke out in a huge grin. "See, that's what I'm talkin' 'bout. A tough girl. You don't seem like you're scurred of nothin'."

"Am I supposed to be *scurred* of you?"

Tonio laughed. "Shoot, while I'm talking to Jaquan, I might need to be hollerin' at you. Why don't *you* come see me? The Blood Brothers can always use a good sister."

Jaquan pulled my arm. "Jasmine, let's go," he demanded.

Tonio laughed again. "I'll see you around, pretty lady. Let's roll," he told his boys.

"A *gang*? You fooling around with a gang?" I asked as we started heading back home.

"Ugggh!" Jaquan groaned, smashing his fist into the palm of his other hand. "Man, I can't believe those dudes."

I shook my head, not believing my brother was messing with a gang. "You don't need to be getting caught up with them, Jaquan."

"I'm not trying to get caught up with them," he said, little lines forming in his forehead, which meant he was getting really mad. "That's the problem."

"So they want you to join their gang?"

He waved me off like he was disgusted, but didn't answer.

"Jaquan," I said, pulling his arm back to get him to stop walking. "I know you're not even thinking about getting involved with a gang? 'Cuz if they don't kill you, Mama will."

"Man, I ain't with no gang," he said, obviously frustrated. "Didn't you just hear me say I'm tryin' to go to college? I'm tryin' to get out of this neighborhood."

"Okay, I was just checkin'."

"Just drop it." We started back to walking.

"Uh-uh," I said. "I'm gonna tell Mama."

"You gonna tell her what? Just keep your big fat mouth shut." He poked his lips out and stomped down the sidewalk. "You make me sick."

I turned up my nose. There was the Jaquan I knew and couldn't stand. But the more I studied him as he walked, the more something didn't seem right. Something in his eyes was different. There was a scared look behind his anger. And that scared me.

I stepped in front of him on the sidewalk, forcing him to stop.

"What are you doing? Move," he said, pushing me aside. Over the past year, my brother had gotten bigger than me, but I was still able to hold my ground against him.

"No. Not until you tell me what's goin' on." I placed my hands on my hips to let him know I was serious.

He sighed heavily before saying, "Look, I just got beef with them, that's all. And I don't want any beef. I just want to handle my business and get out of here. And they're makin' it harder and harder to do that. But I need you to just let me handle this, a'ight? Tonio is a lot of talk, that's all. But stay out of it and please don't bring Mama into it."

I didn't know what to say at first, but finally I nodded before stepping aside. We continued walking home in silence, the fear I felt inside getting worse.

For yourself, your daughter, sister or friend

Check Out These Teen Fiction Titles!